THE PARADOX OF RICHARD III

Who Benefitted from the Impeachment of this British Monarch?

HELLE RINK

The Paradox of Richard III: Who benefited from the impeachment of this English Monarch? by Helle Rink

This book is written to provide information and motivation to readers. Its purpose is not to render any type of psychological, legal, or professional advice of any kind. The content is the sole opinion and expression of the author, and not necessarily that of the publisher.

Printed in the United States of America.

ISBN   978-1-949746-14-3   (Paperback)
ISBN   978-1-949746-15-0   (Digital)

Lettra Press books may be ordered through booksellers or by contacting:
Lettra Press LLC
18229 E 52nd Ave.
Denver City, CO 80249
1 347-903-4909 | info@lettrapress.com
www.lettrapress.com

CONTENTS

To Whose Benefit?

Cui Bono
Marcus Tullius Cicero
Roman advocate and statesman
(BC 106-43)

Marcus Tullius Cicero, in his speech in defense of Sextus Roscius,
accused of parricide (Pro Roscio Amerino). Cicero affirmed that his
client, Sextus Roscius, did not benefit from his father's death but
that others did. Although the 'other' were closed linked to the Roman
dictator of the time (Cornelius Sulla), Cicero won his case.
Cicero attributed the expression 'cui bono' to the Roman consul and
advocate (BC 127), Lucius Cassius Longinus Ravilla, who time
and again asked: 'To whose benefit?' (Cicero won his case).
Cicero also used 'cui bono' in his defense of Tito Annio Milone (Pro
Milone), accused of murdering his political enemy Publius Clodius
Pulcher on the Via Appia outside Rome (BC 52)
(Cicero lost this case).

Richard I *(1157-1199)*

The Plantagenets: "From the Devil we sprung and to the Devil we'll go"

Henry IV *(1366-1399)*

The Beauforts: Legitimated the bastard descendents of John of Lancaster (1340-1399) and Katherine Swynford on the condition that their descendants would never be eligible to inherit the throne of England.

Richard III

"Henry Tydder[i], whereunto he hath [in] no matter interest, right title or colour, as every man well knoweth, for he is descended of bastard blood, for of father side and of mother side..[of his supporters] many be known for open murderers, adulterers and extortioners... every true and natural Englishman born must lay to his hands for his own surety and weal."

To my readers: this book is full of anachronisms.
Don't let it worry you. It's all on purpose.

Introduction

The War of the Roses
(1455-1485)

Two households, both alike in dignity,
From ancient grudge break to new mutiny
Where civil blood makes civil hands unclean.

Yes, of course this is the opening of William Shakespeare's *Romeo and Juliet* but it might as well reflect the basis of the War of the Roses, a civil war that tore Englad apart for years. For the War of the Roses involved two of the most prominent royal families, the houses of York and Lancaster, both descendents of king Edward III (1318-1377) through his second son, Lionel, Duke of York (1338-1368), and his third, John, Duke of Lancaster (1340-1399).

In résumé, John of Lancaster's son, Henry of Bolingbroke, usurped the crown by impeaching King Richard II, son of the Prince of Wales, the Black Prince, and himself a Prince of Wales. Henry Bolingbroke took the crown as Henry IV. When Henry IV died, the crown passed to his son, Henry V, a great warrior who conquered France but died on campaign, leaving the throne to his son, Henry VI, who was then an infant. Henry VI, even as an adult, was a weak king, and the descendants of Lionel of York rose up in rebellion to take the crown, which they claimed was theirs by right through descent from the second, as against the third, son of Edward III (although there was a lady, Philippa of Clarence, between them and Lionel).

This was then was the War of the Roses. The White Rose of York against the Red Rose of Lancaster, which lasted from 1455 to 1471. When it all ended, the side of the White Rose had won and

Edward IV of the White Rose was on the throne. There were no legitimate Lancasters left alive and the Lancastrian heir by default became Henry Tudor, an illegitimate descendant of John of Lancaster through his morganatic marriage to Katherine Swynford as well as an illegitimate descent of Catherine of Valois, widow, of Henry V, through her alliance with the Welshman, Owain Tudor.

When our story opens, Edward IV is new on the throne and the British nobility are not yet sure what to make of him or what his reign will be like and what would be in it for them. Furthermore, Edward had made a very unpopular marriage to the daughter of a knight, Richard Wydville, from what the English nowadays would call the 'landed gentry', certainly neither nobility nor aristocracy. This marriaged didn't go down well, but it had taken place before Edward became king. When he did, the the upper classes were faced with what might be a bitter enemy at court in the form of Queen Elisabeth, née Wydville, now Queen of England, to say nothing of her Wydville family.

So this is where we are.

And when he had opened the fourth seal, and behold a Pale Horse
and his name that sat on him was DEATH.
Revelations 6.7-8

1

The Yorks in Splendour

1.1 Glorious Summer

I found myself lying in my most elegant sphinx position on the balustrade of a terrace at the corner where it turned and sloped downwards following a series of steps leading to a rather shopworn stone lion wearing a crown and holding a shield.

For a few moments, a mist seemed to hang over the landscape but, as I took a closer look, it slowly dissolved. I saw a blue sky with a few fluffy clouds floating lazily around; the air was cool but not unpleasantly so.

As I took in the sights, I saw a garden with all the glorious colors of late spring or early summer. Flowers bloomed, their heads waving gently in the breeze, irresistible to cute yellow and black bees and rainbow colored butterflies. The hedges were neatly trimmed and superbly verdant, the grass mown to perfection. Bushes did what bushes do best in summer: blossom, their flowers filling the air with sweet scents. Birds, too, where out and about, showing off their brilliant summer plumage and doing whatever it is birds do; singing and warbling fit to beat the band. Mating season, what?

Further away, set up beaneath great trees, a gold and silver pavillion had been erected under which large tables had been set up, groaning beneath the best of viands, victuals and wine. Gaily dressed children ran around everywhere, screaming and shouting merrily. The grownups ignored the ruckus, giving their attention to eating and drinking and laughing and arguing. There was a gorgeously dressed man, wearing an enormous amount of jewellery, his cap gay with more feathers than anyone else's. He was huge, whiskered and with the whitest teeth, blond hair and, as far as I could see, blue eyes. Next to him a lady, beautifully dressed in summer green with matching emeralds here, there and everywhere, flowing sleeves and train, a gausemous veil flowing over her golden hair held there by a splendid tiara encrusted with precious stones. The lady of the manor.

Ladies and gentlemen flitted and flirted and a good time was being had by all. A band of sorts, violas, pipes and whatnot, played in the background. Lords and ladies danced; little girls went 'ring a'round the roses' as fast as ever they could, until the lot collided, tripped over each other and collapsed on the grass amid shrieks of laughter.

I sniffed the air and closed my eyes to test the energy levels. Cats can 'see' energy; I see it in shades of white all the way through to black. White, go to sleep. Black, go somewhere else. But here the energy was positive, all white and fluffy, like clouds. Peace! Love! Flower power! I ignored the darker edges.

Lulled by the warmth, I closed my eyes and something made me murmur:

> *"Now is the winter of our discontent*
> *Made glorious summer by this sun of York."*[1]

"What, what?" queried a voice behind me. I looked around, quite upset at having my mellow mood disturbed. A fellow of medium height was leaning against the balustrade a few steps up from my perch. I measured the distance but decided he was too far away to scratch comfortably. So I repeated the lines, swishing my tail which, in cat language, means 'we have not been introduced. Why are you asking me questions? Bugger off.' Of course he couldn't read cat body language so instead he put a finger to his chin and thought for a bit. Then he said:

"This is most wonderful bit poetry and I really like it. It has flow and resonance… But forgive me if I find the meaning somewhat perplexing. Would you be so good as to explain exactly what is meant

---

[1]   *Richard III.* William Shakespeare

by the 'sun of York'? Even a royal family doesn't have its own sun."
I sighed, cat fashion. However, I now knew where I was. Somewhere
in the 15th century. I felt pleased. I had planned my vacation well. The
time of the War of the Roses, after the last battle and way before the
next one. However, my new friend was still waiting for my answer:
he seemed to need everything explained in two letter words.

"My Lord," I said, he must be a lord since he was dressed like
one, "in poetic language, the meaning is: *after a hard [discontented]
winter, the sun [son] of York is shinning.* It has a double meaning, you
see? A pun, you might say." After a few moment, his face cleared and
he said with a loud laugh:

"I see, the sun," pointing upwards, "and the son of York, my
brother Edward over there. How very clever!" So the gentleman
all dolled up was Edward IV and the lady his queen ... offhand, I
couldn't remember her name. My new friend slapped his thighs. I look
at him inquiringly. Was he the king's brother? There were a couple.
George or ... Richard? He seemed to read my mind as he continued:

"But I should introduce myself: I am Richard of Gloucester,
king Edward IV's youngest brother." I may say I was surprised. The
name brought up visions of someone along the lines of Quasimodo,
hunchback, one blind eye and a heart of gold, see Victor Hugo's
Notre Dame de Paris. Fooled again by Will Shakespeare. However,
I let it slide.

"And I," said I, "am Gaius Marius, the cat." Richard beamed.

"Now that we have been introduced, may I ask if you are the
author of those wonderful lines?" Well, I could have lied and swanked
but decided not to.

"Friend of mine." Short and sweet. Richard bit his thumb.

"He must be some poet. Is there more?" Well, there was of course,
lots, lots more but I hoped not to have to go through all of it; as well
as being as long as the old Testament some of it would be plain
embarrassing in present company. So I gave him the two next lines:

"And all the clouds that lour'd upon our house
In the deep bosom of the ocean buried.

He scratched his head. "How can clouds be buried in the ocean?" I closed my eyes and counted to ten. Then I said:

"It's a metaphor, my Lord of Gloucester. It means that yesterday's problems have all gone away. The ocean is by way of poetic license." Will Shakespeare, the king of poetic license.

Richard's face lightened up.

"Of course, metaphors. I see now. Good, good, what comes next?" I continued:

> *"Now are our brows bound with victorious wreaths;*
> *Our bruised arms hung up for monuments;*
> *Our stern alarums changed to merry meetings,*
> *Our dreadful marches to delightful measures."*

He lifted his fingers in the air as if checking off a list:

"We are victorious, hence the wreaths, our armour and weapons, worn and cracked from long use, have been put away as we don't need them anymore and instead of battles we have social gatherings and dancing." He looked at me delighted. I nodded.

"That's it exactly." I wanted to pat him on the back but this wasn't possible, given the differences in our specifications. He made a movement with his hand that I interpreted as wanting me to continue. I did but swore this would be the last bit.

> *"Grim-visaged war hath smooth'd his wrinkled front;*
> *And now, instead of mounting barded steeds*
> *To fright the souls of fearful adversaries,*
> *He capers nimbly in a lady's chamber*
> *To the lascivious playing of a lute."*

Well, I've told Will these lines were a bit off-colour but Will likes a bawdy bit here and there. What it really meant, of course, that Will had no time for Edward IV. Richard went back to his imaginary list.

"The wars have ceased and we no longer need to be constantly on our war horses, scaring our enemies to death, he…" Richard frowned: "He? Who is he?"

"Dunno," I said. "But whoever 'he' is, he sure likes the ladies." Richard laughed merrily:

"Must be my brother, Edward; he was always one for the skirts. Couldn't see a one without chasing it." He raised his eyebrows in question mode. "Is there any more?"

"No," I said firmly, "that's it." Richard said in a dreamy kind of voice:

"I'd sure like to meet your friend. I am a great enthusiast for poetry – in fact, I think education should be encouraged in all classes of society." He looked serious and bit his finger in a thoughtful kind of way. "Education, not commerce, will make this a great nation."

I wasn't going to disabuse him. Piracy and stealing, not commerce or education, would make this a great nation. But, as the man says, it takes all sorts. He sat down on one of the lower steps close to my perch and heaved a sigh of contentment.

"But your friend the poet is right. This is indeed a new beginning, a happy beginning, for my family and for England." Well, that might be; the common folk would just be glad not to have knights trampling all over their fields and chasing their livestock. For the humans at the bottom of the food chain, it matters little whether the king's family name is Lancaster or York. If they had any sense, they'd get rid of the lot and have a republic, where the bastards can be thrown out every four years. But it seems the English cannot live without their monarchy, no matter how loutish, stupid, greedy and boorish its members may be. As I always say, there's no telling for taste. Richard went on in a dreamy sort of voice:

"You know, I have never lived in a world at peace." I wanted to ask: *who has?* Since the first humanoid picked up the first stone and found he could use it to hit another humanoid over the head, inflicting damage or death, war has been a constant on planet Earth. But my pal sounded sad, as if he'd missed something that was everyone else's birthright.

"I've been in exile twice, you know. This," and he swept his arm around, encompassing, if you like, the whole gathering, "is by way of being a restoration party." He scraatched his chin. "In a way I can count myself lucky; I was born too late for the big battles and when I was old enough there were just two more to be fought: Barnet and then Tewkesbury that ended the War of the Roses and made Edward king." I sniffed:

"All to the good since it got rid of three kings and eight dukes. The world would be all the better with less kings and dukes."

Richard didn't respond. He was probably trying to figure out who the three kings were. I didn't know myself; read it somewhere. Silence reigned until I broke it:

"Made quite a name for yourself, didn't you, at Tewkesbury? Breaking the Lancastrian center. Our hero!" Richard didn't see the sarcasm but tried to look modest.

"One does," he said, humble-like, "what has to be done." I lifted my head and sniffed the summer air.

"The War of the Roses. Such a pretty name," I said, adding nastily, "for covering up such unholy ambition and greed." Richard frowned and I said: "The Red Horse rode forth and his name was civil strife, the cruelest of them all."[ii] Richard gave me a sideways look and frowned.

"But we, the Yorkists, had right on our side. Our claim was the truest." I rolled my eyes.

"Puuleese, don't give me that. The only reason the war ever happened was because Henry VI was a weak king and easily challenged. Had your lot faced Henry V or even Henry IV, you would have kept your heads down and cultivated your gardens." Richard didn't seem to want to get into this discussion.

"You're just a cat," he said with finality. "What do you know? And, anyway, Henry VI might have been weak but his wife, Margaret d'Anjou, wasn't. She gave us a good run for our money." Thinks I: had she been a man, she'd have beat the lot of you from here all the way to Sunday. But I let it go. No use arguing once it's all over. I changed the subject:

"So," I asked, "now that all is peace and love, what are you going to do?" With a dreamy look in his eyes, he said:

"I shall marry the Lady Anne." I raised my whiskers in surprise:

"You mean the Lady Anne who was married to Edward, the Prince of Wales, son of Henry VI? The daughter of Warrick, the kingmaker?"

"Who else?" he cried. "The lady is widowed and will need a husband. And having been on the losing side of the war, she will also want a protector." I said carefully:

"They do say that you were the one who killed her husband." Richard shook his head.

"Nonsense. In that mêlée, anyone may have killed anyone. I can't swear I didn't but then I don't remember specifically that I did. That last battle is all a haze. Ahh, look, there is Lady Anne, alone on a bench over by the rose garden. I shall go and press my suit at once."

And off he went, on courtship bent. Perhaps not a very sensitive soul, our Richard. But then, I shouln't forget that marriages, in those days, were not made in heaven but at the conference table. Perhaps Anne hadn't even loved Edward, Prince of Wales. At least, here she was, at the victors' garden party.

I lay my head down on my paws and watched Richard as he walked across the lawn and sat down on the stone bench next to Lady Anne. Stealthily, he moved ever closer and closer to her while she edged away until the poor lady was pushed off the bench altogether and onto the grass. Richard hastily picked her up and helped her brush off dead leaves and such from her skirts. I couldn't help murmuring to myself:

> *Was ever woman in this humour woo'd?*
> *Was ever woman in this humour won?*

But Anne seemed to take it all as good sport, laughed, and Richard did too, he took her arm and put it through his and they ambled off into the sunlit garden.

Servants ran to and from the palace with laden and/or empty trays. As two of them passed, one going, the other coming, I heard a whisper:

"Look out for that cat, Tom. He steals. Swiped half a salmon from my tray." I licked my paws for the last traces of salmon, cleaned my face, cat fashion, and straightened my whiskers. The other servant said:

"Queer looking beast, not like our tabby at home. A cat with blue eyes. It ain't natural, Rob! And look at the size of the thing." I gave him a gimlet look with my blue eyes and he scampered off. I am a Siamese cross; I have the correct Siamese dark markings on head, paws and tail, but my back has brown fur, which is where the 'cross' comes in. I would never win any prizes in a Siamese catshow. Anyhow, cross or not, Siamese cats were not a familiar sight at that time or in that place. I sighed with satisfaction, thinking life was good and that a snooze was in order. Cats are always fully aware of what's going on around them even when asleep; it's called 'catnap' and that's how they've survived and thrived for six million years. I stretched out, turned on my side, sighed contently and was out like a light.

I woke up to find Richard next me.

"Well," he said, "seeing it was a first attempt, I think I've made considerable progress. The lady owns just about the whole of the north of England." I looked shocked.

"I thought you loved her!"

"Of course I do," was his affronted answer, "but I love her so much more with all those estates. We shall be married and go back north – I am governor of the North, you know. Keep the Scots in their place – on the other side of the border. We shall do very well, Anne and I." Well, I had seen a lot of positive energy surrounding them so he might be right. I had a good long stretch and washed my face.

So we sat there, enjoying the end of the afternoon, saying nothing but somehow communicating. Being a cat, there was much I could 'read' of Richard's moods as shadows flew across his face. A quiet man, a faithful man (given the right circumstances) a brave man (if at all necessary). I yawned. Yes, a nice guy – all things being equal. I asked:

"Why are you sitting here with a cat? Why aren't you over there with your kinfolk, whooping it up and having about a dozen drinks?" I got a sidelong glance and a cough.

"Truth to tell, I don't really get on with my family. I mean, they're kin and deserve support and so on."

"I see," was my comment. "If you must." He didn't answer but went on:

"As for my brother the King's in-laws, the least said about them the better." Oh! "The North," he continued, nodding his head vigorously, "that's the place for me." Well, indeed, you couldn't get farther from London without ending up in the Isle of Skye.

The evening following that wonderful summer day was magnificent – though none of the humans seemed to notice. Dusk was falling and that, especially over parkland, is always beautiful. Birds doing their evening toilet. Tree branches sighing in the soft wind. Flowers nodding their heads lazily, waiting for the dew that would refresh them. In fact, *When all of nature pleases and only man is vile* [2]. The lengthening shadows always give me a frisson, a moment of mystery and magic.

I.2 In the Drawing Room

The sun set and evening shadows fell, and the party decided to go indoors, led by the Queen.

"It's so hot out here," she said, fanning herself with a golden shawl. "I shall order tea and refreshments in the drawing room. I think we've had all the fresh air we need for today." And so the procession moved onto the long terrace, through what looked like French doors and settled down as they liked. Flunkies appeared with the necessities for continued existence. There was tea and sandwiches and cake; usual stuff. On a table discreetly in the background, decanters and bottles were placed – for the gentlemen, who headed towards it as if drawn by a magnet.

I noticed that the white positive energy was turning somewhat grey, with easily definable black countours; so, not wanting to miss any of the squabbles that were sure to ensue, I followed the crowd and curled up, as comfortably as only a cat can, on a mantelpiece, licking a paw or two.

My eyes went over the assemblied party. The queen, I had learned, had been borne Elisabeth Wydville, married Lord John Grey, now deceased, with whom she had two sons, Lords Grey and Dorset. Then Edward of York, the future IV, cast his eyes on her and she made sure there was a ring on her finger before he took them off again. She and Edward had a whole slew of kids, two sons, Edward, Prince of Wales, and Richard, plus uncounted daughter. Another important member

---

[2]   Reginald Heber (1783-1826)

of her family was Lord Rivers, her brother. Let it be said that queen Elisabeth was a very devoted mother and sister.

A flunky of sorts came to the terrace door and announced:

"His Grace, the duke of Buckingham[iii] and the Earl of Derby[iv]." These gentlemen presented themselves, all smiles and bows.

My Lord Buckingham was a richly dressed tall heavy-set man not in his first youth. His hair, originally dark brown, was turning grey and starting to recede. His brown eyes were piggy-sized and he had the unnerving habit of peering at you through slits. I later decided he must have been very short sighted. He had all the qualities of a thug, covered by a thin veneer of gentility, manners and fine clothes.

Lord Derby was elderly, corpulent, I think they call it, moon faced, with a couple of chins, hair mere wisps of memory, but a kindly face. The size of his nose was in fair proportion to the rest of him; in contrast, he had thin lips, pale blue eyes that never seemed to fix themselves on anything but moved nonstop from point to point. I wouldn't have trusted either of them as far as I could throw a cat. But then, I should blame the times more than individuals, for keeping one's head on one's neck required eternal vigilance.

Earl Rivers, the queen's brother, jumped up to do the honors.

"My Lords Buckingham and Derby You are most welcome." The two put on their best courtier smiles, sweeping deep bows, first to the Queen then to the assembly and said, almost in unison:

"Good evening to your Royal Grace! And your family. And such a handsome family it is."

"May your future days be as full of joy, your Majesty, as this glorious summer has been." Lord of cats, bring me the sick bag. The Queen did not seem impressed for she smiled coldly. Lord Derby was married to Margaret Beaufort[v], the mother of the Lancastrian pretender, Henry Tudor, son of her first husband, Edmund Tudor, Earl of Richmond. Although in Brittany with her son, the shadow of that formidable lady seemed to have followed her poor husband because Elisabeth answered with undisguised bitterness in her voice:

"I don't think your lady wife would endorse your good wishes, my Lord Derby. A proud arrogant woman, my Lady Derby, and no friend to me. But, in spite of your connection to her, I bear you no ill will." Now, that sounded very noble and would have made me run a mile but Derby gave a merry – although rather hollow – laugh.

"Oh, my good your Grace, you must not take seriously the envious tittle tattle and rumours spread by lowborn slanderers. Perhaps one can attribute her want of sweetness to her constant anxieties for her son Henry and their prolonged exile abroad. I assure you it is nothing, nothing that signifies; my Lady holds your Grace in high esteem. Why, she thinks of you quite as a sister." I began to suspect Derby was not as stupid as he looked; perhaps he had a one way ticket to Brittany in his back pocket.

The Wydvilles exchanged covert glances. All this talk of envious tittle-tattle and lowborn slanderers may have hit a few marks but there was no way the Wydvilles could fight it without becoming self-accusatory. Me, I would have invoked the Fifth[vi]. The newcomers were offered tea but, not surprisingly, preferred the drinks table.

Everyone having been served, the Queen asked not anyone in particular:

"And how did you find the King today?" A curious question as it implied the Queen had no first hand news of her husband. Not surprising, perhaps, given Edward IV's predilection for gading about. Buckingham answered, all kindness and bonhommie:

"Full of spirits, indeed, my lady, jovial and in love with all the world. And his greatest wish is that we should all be reconciled: his brothers, Clarence and Gloucester, your brother and sons and the older nobility, such as myself, and my very dear friend here, Lord Derby. A pious wish and so like the king not to think of himself but of the good of the realm."

I lifted my head a mite. Well, well. Peace and goodwill to all men. Bring on the violins. The Queen rose and began walking backwards and forwards, wringing her hands, her forehead a mass of frowns.

"I wish such a reconciliation were indeed possible but our differences may run so deep not even the king's wishes can bridge them. I am afraid the height of our happiness was this one glorious summer and will not come again."

Lord Hastings[vii] was then announced and joined the gathering of the best friends but the undercurrents revealed as the bitterest of enemies. After the usual courtesies, bows and scrapings, the newcomener was offered drinks, Lord Hastings going for a stiff whisky and soda. There was a period of chitchat, weather and so on.

Then Richard arrived, accompanied by another gentleman, tall, blonde and muscular – and loud. I decided this must be George, Duke of Clarence. The two bowed and smiled to the whole party. Unsurprisingly, their presence put a further damper on the party. Richard had a glass of wine and Clarence a stiff whisky and soda and almost fell over when he saw Lord Rivers.

"My dear Lord Rivers," he cried out, arms wide open. "My old comrade in arms!" and gave the man a bear hug. Rivers did not look pleased. I wonder which side Clarence was referring to. The white rose or red? Since they'd fought on both sides.

Richard then turned his back to the nobility and addressed the Wydville clan through the Queen:

"I hear, my Lady Queen, that you consider me to be your enemy. Really, I fail to understand why I merit such abuse. What is the reason? Why, we have been allies and fellow travellers, have we not, on the long road that led us through dark days to triumph, victory and the crown! Yet you, Madam, complain of me to the King. I who wish to live a simple life, doing harm to no one, cannot but wonder why baseless innuendo is spread about me!" Clarence, nodded his head, smiling.

"My sentimens exactly! Well said, Richard!" Both very sensible, of course, and the Wydvilles were naturally furious. Lord Grey, that young hothead, jumped to his feet and cried out haughtily to Richard:

"And to whom do you address such accusations, my Lord of Gloucester?" Richard, who had taken off his cap and was twirling it around one finger, replied pleasantly:

"My dear Lord Grey, and any of you gentlemen present, should the cap fit you not, why, I am speaking to none of you." George grinned. It seemed to me that, in the area of wit, Richard was oodles ahead of George. Another silence during which looks passed between the various parties. George took the opportunity and continued:

"It is our duty to sustain our brother the king with cheerful care and not bedevil him with lamentations and complaints. He already carries a very heavy load." The remark about caps was still floating around so there were no comments. Then the Queen spoke:

"My dear brothers Gloucester and Clarence, you misread us all. Indeed you do. It is the King himself, without any encouragement from myself or my family, who desires that you both explain, quite freely,why you dislike me and those close to me." Richard threw his arms open as if to embrace the lot of them and cried:

"But there is nothing to explain, my dear sister!" He turned to Clarence, "Is there, my brother?" Clarence shook his head vigourously. Richard continued: "My brother and I bear none of you ill will; in fact, I stand your fast friend and supporter, as I have always done. The Wydvilles have a history of being good gentlefolk and loyal vassals. Although your father, my Lady, did at one time support Henry VI." Oops… "But that is understandable, quite understandable." Well, Richard was cleverer than I had thought. Amid arrows and stones, nothing seemed to touch him or anger him. George bowed to everyone.

"I do, I do indeed agree with my brother Richard. And I myself know how it is to be on the wrong side, according to some, and how difficult it is to know whether might is right or right is might." My head swam. Then, Richard put his arm around the shoulders of the Duke of Buckingham. "My Lord Buckingham, I am sure, will agree with me and my brother George, wil you not, and you, Lord Derby, and of course, Lord Hastings."

"Indeed," quoth Buckingham, with another bow: "always your servant, Madame."

"And I," chimed in Derby and Hastings as a Greek chorus. Richard then addressed the Queen directly, with a pleading look in his eyes and his hands folded as if in prayer:

"It is I who have come to beseech you, your Grace. Indulgence for those members of our oldest and most loyal nobility who are held in contempt at court and disgraced for no known reason. See Lord Hastings, so lately restorred to us from the Tower!" George put his arm around Hastings, who very quickly assumed a sad and mortified expression. Elizabeth, drawing herself up to her full height and she was tall for women at that time, answered haughtily:

"My Lords Gloucester and Clarence, Lord Hastings well knows who was responsible for his release." Hastings' eyes looked daggers and I could hear him thinking, 'yeah, after putting me there.'

Richarid said sorrowfully: "Have I ever declared, as I know others have, that you were instrumental of sending poor Lord Hastings to the Tower so that your brother," he bowed to Lord Rivers, "could become governor of Calais?" No comments from those present. George then took over:

"Of advancing your sons to high positions at court and then denying having done so? Why, we all understand that you should seek support and guidance from those closest to you, your own kith and kin." He let go of Lord Hastings and attempted to embrace the Queen but she was having none of it.

"Sir," she said, stepping away from him, "I have had enough of both your malice and slanders and taunts. I will not endure it! I will not! I will not!" Richard looked at her sorrowfully as well he might. George, too, assumed a look of deep regret. From where I lay, I didn't know what Richard was guilty of, though I wouldn't put anything past George or Buckingham, if either thought it safe. Derby didn't need to do any slandering as his wife, Margaret Beaufort, was so good at it. Richard faced the Queen, sighing and said sorrowfully:

"And will you say as much to the King, driving a wedge between him and his brothers, both of whom love him dearly as brothers should, and are his most loyal servants!" Deep sigh from the two brother and Clarence continued:

"Do not, my lady, be so unwomanly, unmerciful and uncharitable!" He turned to Richard and the other three cronies:

"Gentlemen, I ask you humbly to assure the Queen that you have never heard either myself or my brother Richard speak of her as anything but our dearest sister."

"Oh, what nonsense," cried Richard.

"Never!" roared Buckingham.

"Unthinkable!" chimed Derby.

"Unimaginable," added Hastings. Derby then took his leave, scraping and bowing and I bet a month's cat food he was straight for Waterloo Station and the Eurostar.

Richard resumed, his hands behind his back, head lowered:

"I bear you no grudge, my lady, and you have my full sympathy for the slaying of your father at the battle of St Albans fighting in Queen Margaret's army; you, Lord Rivers, where by his side, as a dutiful son should." Every Wydville flew up and opened his or her mouth. George held up his hands:

"Peace, peace my friends. Whatever happened in the past stays in the past; let it all forgotten." But Lord Rivers shouted furiously:

"My Lord Dukes, we have always been faithful to our sovereign Lord as we would be faithful to either of you, should one of you become king!"At this, Richard cried out in horror:

"Me, a king? Heaven forbid! I would rather be a pedlar!" George smiled behind his hand but said nothing. Penny for your thoughts, George. Richard. shook his head and shaded his eyes with his hand. "All this arguing distresses me. I shall return to Yorkshire since I can do no good here." Bowing, he left and I sprinted after him. George stayed behind for another drink.

1.3 Family Life

The early days of Edward IV's second reign was peaceful[viii]; not surprising since both the nobility and the commons were exhausted and needed a break from battles and general mayhem.

In fact, it was all so quiet I decided to stay around for a while. Richard and Anne had a grand wedding and went off to enjoy married bliss in Yorkshire and I went along for the long and awful ride, in dreadful carts with no springs, over bad roads, full of ruts when it was dry and mud when it was not. A terrible place, England. No wonder they thirsted for an empire where the weather might be more predictable. But all that came later.

Once in the North, Richard and Ann and their retinue moved into Middleham Manor or Castle; like all such places, the rooms, even the best of them, were nasty, damp and full of unpleasant smells and wiggly creatures. I wrinkled my nose in disgust. No proper drainage. I never went near the kitchen; just the thought of it was enough to bring up my last meal.

The main dining hall was particularly awful. The rushes on the floor soaked up spilled wine and food. Diners threw gnawed bones on the floor and Richard's gy-enormous hunting dogs fought over every scrap – almost to the death. Disgusting! Dogs are such scavengers!

No proper idea of hygiene. But I did rid the second story, where the living quarters were, of mice and rats and cats – all of whom, I'm sure, had no end to nasty diseases.

Needless to say, there were also an untold number of kittens and to get rid of them was a major undertaking. Kittens have unbounded energy, they are cute, cuddly and adorable – I'm sure it's all part of a cat's genetic profile – they know it and use it. I chased them all over the castle but the more I got down to the stables, the more there seemed to be. I could have killed a few *pour*, as the man said, *encourager les autres*[ix].

But it's also part of an adult cat's built-in instincts not to kill kittens, no matter how ubiquitous or intolerably they behave, or the *cattus* species would have been wiped out eons ago. And kittens know it too, which makes them smug and think they have the right to chase your tail, steal your food and your favorite nap spaces. After an exhausting few days, I decided my only option was to become an alpha male. Cats aren't hierarchical but it can be done, with lots of hissing and cat body language. At last the job was done and I think I must have slept for a week. But I always suspected a kitten had slipped through my net. I used to glimpse a white streak shimmer by but, dammit, I never managed to catch it.

I then looked for the warmest, coziest and most comfortable nook in the place, which I decided was in Richard's study, and rarely left it.

Anne at first objected to my coming North at all; she disapproved of cats in beds and on furniture – and given what her bed was like, full of creepy crawlies, I couldn't agree more. No cat in his right mind would put up with it. Richard just laughed and I sniggered.

However, once she saw my home improvements in the matter of mice and rats, the odd cockroach and feral cats, she became quite friendly. She soon learnt that leaving furs or warm capes lying around unattended inevitably resulted in finding a cat inside – or the garment covered in cat fur – when she needed it. But, as I told her, this should teach her maids not to leave valuable furs lying around but to put things away tidily.

And so, as in all fairy stories, a bouncing baby came along. Little Edward of Middleham. Anne was very nervous about me and little

Edward. She pleaded with Richard not to let me into the baby's nursery.

"He might," she said anxiously, "lie on the baby and smother him. One hears such tales." I giggled. Richard laughed and gave Anne a hug.

"Soul of my soul," he said, "whoever Gaius loves, he loves not babies. He won't go anywhere near Eddie, afraid he'll pick up some disease or other." Anne blanched. But Richard went on: "So calm down." Instead of calming down, Anne was quite offended.

"Eddie's a lovely baby!" She huffed. "Everybody says so."

"And so Gaius will love Eddie in his own way but at a distance. If he catches a rat crawling into the cradle, that rat will never see another tomorrow." That improved her mood and I got a soulful look.

"Well, in that case…" she trailed off. I took the chance to add touches of my own for streamlining the nursery, ordering the nanny and maids around:

"The nursery must be nice, clean, comfy and warm. The nanny and nurse maids must wash their hands before handling Eddie. Before a change of nappy, he should be washed with clear water and be wrapped in a spanking clean warmed diaper." The nurses didn't look pleased but said nothing because Richard added:

"Why, that sounds very sensible, ladies. I hope you will all follow the advice – if you wish to continue in our household." General grumbling but since Middleham was a good billet, no one really wanted to leave.

"And, oh, yes," I added, for there was something I had forgotten. "Be sure to air the room thoroughly every day – you can take Eddie elsewhere while it's being done. And no putting him back in a crib with soiled or wet bedclothes."

And so, having added my little bit about housekeeping and baby care, I went to sleep by the fire.

From a bouncing baby, little Eddie became a toddler, then walked, talked, and made Middleham Castle a hell for man and beast. He was everywhere. He wanted to know everything. He loved cats and since there was only one in residence, no matter where I went or how cunningly I hid myself, I always heard the pitter patter of little feet behind me. Eddie would fall over me. He would step on my tail and, bless me, step on my paws, which is the very worst thing you can do to a cat because it's excrutiatingly painful. Chez moi, after such an accident I would retire under the bed but if you did that in Medieval England, you took your life in your hands. The filth, odds and ends and creatures who lived there were undescribable! Oh, and Eddie also pulled my ears, earning him a scratch that made him howl. But even the scratch did not stop him. He would gambol around hollering:

"Kitty, Kitty…" Till I seriously considered bringing back some of the cats I had exiled to the stables.

He tried to drag me around with him, with my back legs dragging on the floor. But I put a stop to that. One scratch and we were all good. Of course, Eddie would scream and the head nurse would come running, wagging a finger at me, which I took as an invitation to bite, after which she changed direction screaming, blood dripping on the floor, Eddie in her arms. Sorry, I'm sure, but one most impose respect. After that, we were all friends.

Richard's main job was to keep the Scots in order, who lived just across the border and always made infernal nuisances of themselves, raiding cattle and stealing sheep. One might as well have been in the wild west. Anne and Richard also did a lot of community services through what he termed his Council of the North, of which he was extremely proud. I think he founded King's and Queen's Colleges at Cambridge but confess I wasn't too interested. Whatever time they had left was spent cooing and playing with Eddie. At least it got Eddie off my back.

So time passed as time will. Summer came as summer does in England, a day at a time, and little Eddie and I played on the lawn – he chased me and I chased him. No prizes for guessing who won. He also liked something akin to primitive football. I found this very tiresome until I discovered that, if I hit the ball while it was still in the air, it would go off on a tangent with Eddie chasing it like mad while I napped.

2
George of Clarence

2.1 Into the Tower

And then the bomb fell, so as to speak. A letter from Buckingham informed Richard that his brother, George, Duke of Clarence, had been imprisoned in the Tower. This was late in the year so Twelth Night and New Year passed in a desultory fashion; no one at Middleham was in a party spirit.

And then Richard was recalled to court. He decided that, along with servants, secretaries, archers and so forth, I should come with him, with Anne and little Eddie staying at home. So Richard and I made the long dreary journey in a rattling old coach. I dreamed of the trains that would one day carry people from York to London in about 2 hours and where you could buy cups of tea and bits of chocolate. But I said nothing. That was too far in the future. I asked Richard:

"Why did you leave Anne at Middleham?" He raised an eyebrow.

"Really, Gaius, for a smart cat, you are pretty stupid." I gulped:

"You're right, Richard. Never allow hostages to fortune."

"Bingo!" And Richard went back to his papers.

Once in London, Richard unloaded me and staff at Baynard's Castle that also contained Richard's mother, the Duckess of York, who was sort of, but not quite, in Holy Orders. I'd been there before and hadn't missed the place after I left. It was gloomy with rooms at weird angles and corridors and stairs that didn't seem to lead anywhere. Typical of the period! Richard barked at me:

"Don't you go off anywhere! I need a word with my mother. Then you and I are going to Happy Hour at the Palace." Sometimes saying 'no' is just so much wasted energy so when he came back for me I followed him through the garden and down to the dock where a private barge was waiting and we got in – myself, most unwillingly – and headed upstream as our dwelling was on the wrong end and side of the river from Whitehall.

As Richard entered the great hall, Queen Elizabeth rose to greet him with a show of very little pleasure and a sigh or two. This lady never stopped moaning. The queen, in spite of all those children and the fact that she was getting on a bit, was still a good looking woman, her figure trim and she obviously took care of her clothes and face.

The whole family – at least the whole Wydville gang – was there, and gloomy faces were ten a penny. I closed my eyes to take in the room's level of energy. There was a variety of negativity, from lighter to darker shades of grey created by fear, belligerence, ambition and cunning, just what you would expect in a room full of people not sanguine about their futures.

After a sister-brother-in-law kiss, she looked down at me, drawing her silk skirts back:

"Who brought this cat in? I detest cats!" Richard opened his eyes wide:

"Madam, forgive me, I was given to understand you were especially fond of them." He picked me up. "A fine specimen of a feline; I would have brought a black one but it seems black cats are scarce on the market! I believe there is, at present, a great demand for them!" I scratched him and he dropped me. Why give the lady ideas.

2.2 In the Presence of the Enemy

The Queen sighed deeply again, sat down and leaned back in her chair, closed her eyes, a scented handkerchief against her forehead. Richard swept his eyes around the assembled party:

"I see your whole family is here. Oh, and my mother apologizes for not joining us; you must understand, she now has my brother

George's children to look after." The queen fanned herself with her handkerchief and said in a sad voice:

"The poor little ones! How I feel for them!" The hypocrite! "Having so many of my own, I know how precious each one is!"

"Indeed," snarled Richard. "No mother! No father! What is to become of them?" The Queen answered.

"Indeed, indeed; my brother! One can only pray that heaven will provide." An early version, I would think, of 'let them eat cake'.

Richard then greeted the Wydville retinue: brother, Earl Rivers, sons, Dorset and Grey. There were also assorted aunts, uncles, cousins once- and twice removed but Richard didn't bother with them. He turned again to the Queen:

"My dear sister, I was hoping to see my brother, the king. Is he not joining us?"

"Of course," she answered listlessly, "I cannot imagine what is keeping him." She waved at various servants hanging about. "Please serve our guests with whatever they desire." Most of the gentlemen went for whiskey while the ladies indulged in rosé wine. No one offered me anything so I scratched Richard's leg. He jumped a bit and summoned a servant girl.

"Will you please provide my cat with some water? Fresh from the pump, mind you!" The girl bobed a curtsey and the water she brought in a soup plate was actually not too bad, though not Perrier. I lapped it up. Socializing is thirsty work.

And then, as if in a whilrlwind, the king arrived, followed by various lackeys, aides and so on. I saw Lord Hastings among them. Richard had told me that Lord Hastings was an old friend of the king's, adept at arranging for ladies and other goodies as the king might require. He still looked wan and pale from his holiday in the Tower.

The king threw his cloak off in a careless sort of way, assured that someone would catch it and put it away neatly, as someone duly did. He was a large imposing man although he had seen better days. Perhaps Hastings' troubles were not the quality of his wares but the king's ability to perform. Blame the messenger! The king bellowed:

"My dear brother Richard, what a surprise! Welcome, welcome! And why do you keep yourself innured in the North? We never see you at all!" Turning to the Queen: "Isn't that so, Elisabeth? How often have I said to you – why isn`t my brother Richard at court! We miss him sorely, do we not?" Unenthusiastic murmurs from those present. Richard bowed to Edward who then gave him a big hug.

"My dearest brother and sovereign lord," was Richard's answer with something like steel in his voice. "I am sure you understand that my commitments in the North, what with keeping our borders with Scotland safe, leaves me very little spare time for social calls. However, on this ocassion, I came to you about a matter that is close to my heart – and I hope to yours. The fate of our brother George." Edward's face turned to stone. Richard plowed on:

"I was hoping you, Sire, could tell me why our brother George is in the Tower! You will understand that our mother is much distressed!" He hesitated before continuing: "My Lord Brakenbury, Lord Lieutenant of the Tower, tells me that, on your orders, no one is allowed access to my brother! Not even me!" Edward drew himself up. I could read his fury! He was the king! How dare anyone question his decisions – as wrong as they might be! He put on his most haughty look and looked down his nose. He was, after all, a tad taller than Richard.

"I can't understand your problem, brother Richard, you know those incarcerated in the Tower are there on express orders of the King!" Richard cleared his throat.

"It's not anyone nor is it no one; it's our brother George! What on earth is going on? Why can't I see him?" I looked at Edward and he seemed ready to have a heart attack. He looked at Richard and his nostrils flared and literally spouted flames. Edward had been handsome in his day, blonde, blue eyes and so on, but now, although still a sight to be seen, his hair was receding and had a dead, stringy look to it besides being flecked with dirty gray; the blue eyes were faded and bloodshot; Edward liked his booze. He was also starting to run to fat. He shouted at Richard:

"Did you not hear? Are you deaf? The King! The King has sent Clarence to the Tower!"

Richard stared him down:

"Why, Edward…" but got no further as the king turned on him like a tiger and bellowed:

"Your Majesty to you, my lord to you, your Grace to you, or have you forgotten I am king and your suzerain?" Richard went on gamely.

"Yes, my Lord, but you are also my brother. And you are George's brother too. Why, just think what we three have been through together and how we have fought, lost loved ones, to see our dreams come true in this new golden age, with you as King and our succor!" In answer to this call for brotherly love and gratitude – and I could have told Richard he was wasting his breath to say nothing of his credibility – Edward roared.

"George! My brother!" His voice dripped contempt. "This lying cheating treasonous traitorous scheming creature; were he three times my brother, to the Tower he would go because in the Tower he belongs! And his name begins with G!" Richard gave a nasty laugh.

"Indeed, my Lord! His name begins with G. G for George, or, if you like, G for Gloucester or G for Gaius." Edward stared at him.

"Gaius? Who's Gaius?" Richard bellowed at him:

"Gaius is my sodding cat! My Lord! Are you going to incarcerate him too?" This was nasty and I hid under a sofa. Richard continued, having now completely lost it.

"Are you going to execute every person in the kingdom whose name begins with G? By God, you have a son named George!" The whole conversation was obviously getting out of hand. Edward and Richard were puffing away, trying to get their bearings. Richard was the first to recover:

"Tell me, what does a name beginning with G have to do with anything?" He ground his teeth. "It's that evil witch, working through the Wydville woman…" Edward sneered:

"You mean the Queen?" Richard staggered on:

"I understand the Queen has dreams and she confides to her husband – you, Edward! Have you now, under her guiding hand, taken to believing in portents and wizardry and such like? I understand that one of my Lady's latest dreams sent your best friend, my Lord Hastings, to the Tower. Has another dream revealed treason by a person whose name begins with G!" This sounded so ridiculous that Edward seemed to return to his senses. He clapped Richard on the shoulder.

"My dear brother, I am afraid this is all a misunderstanding. Yes, George is in the Tower but who says he must stay there? Trust me, brother Richard, and all may still be well." Edward turned and bowed to the company, who bowed back. Without a further glance at anyone, he marched out. But Richard caught him at the door. He dropped on one knee.

"Edward, my brother, my liege, my friend. Promise me, for both our sakes and for our mother, that you will not harm George. For all his faults, remember that in the eyes of God we too may have our share of them; he is our brother and our mother's son." Edwards stopped, turned towards Richard, smiled, patted his cheeks and left without a word.

Richard rose to his feet, turned and left the hall and I sneaked after him.

We returned to Baynard's Castle where the old Duchess of York was waiting impatiently for news. She clung to Richard as soon as he appeared.

"Tell me, my son. How do matters stand?" Richard stroked her hand gently.

"Not good, mother."

"But surely," sobbed the Duchess, "there must be some pity in Edward's heart for his poor brother." Richard hugged her.

"Mother, Edward's heart is no longer in Edward's bosom. I have done what I could and I cannot do more. We must now leave it in the hands of God." The poor old lady sank onto a chair of sorts, Richard called for wine. I crept into a corner. I mean, a mother cat may eat (ugh) a deformed kitten although I have known exceptions. But no mother cat will destroy a grown kitten – mainly, I suppose, because she'll have forgotten that he's hers and he will become a public nuisance if some human doesn't think he's cute and takes him in.

The old Duchess, although much distressed, had lived long enough to know that anything can happen and usually did. So she sniveled and said sorrowfully:

"It was the proposed marriage, you know, Richard, which made Edward angry."

"I heard something of that," he answered, "Mary, Duchess of Burgundy, wasn't it?" The Duchess nodded. "A very powerful lady, a very rich lady," continued Richard. "Yes, I can see how that would not suit Edward at all." I closed my eyes and dreamed: in my mind I saw George with a great Burgandian army invading England and taking the throne from Edward. I suppose Edward saw this too.

Later, in his chamber, Richard threw himself on the bed and I curled up on the softest of the pillows, after giving it a thorough pummeling. Richard did not look too pleased at this treatment of his mother's property but, to give him his due, he just glared at me before opening the conversation.

"Well, Gaius. I confess that giving Edward the right about made me feel slightly better." I shivered. Duck walking over my grave? I stretched out.

"Hope you won't come to regret it; Edward has improsined one brother and obviously plans to kill him; the next one will be easier." He glared at me but then said in a decided tone:

"You know something, Gaius, I don't care. Let him do his worst. I really don't want to live in his kind of world."

I stayed quietly at Barnyard while Richard rushed from pillar to post, seeking support for George. He would have taken me along, too, had I not hidden in a deep dark closet.

A few days later, without a word, he bundled his things and me into the cart-carriage and we went back to the North.

In mid-January Richard was informed that a session of Parliament had been called to pass judgment on Clarence. Myself, I was surprised he hadn't died during the winter. I've heard conditions at the Tower were truly terrible, damp and cold, to say nothing of the rack and thumbscrews.

Not surprising, word came that Parliament had voted attainder against George, which meant that all his goods and possessions went to the crown, with George condemned to death. It never rains but it pours. Anne wailed her heart away.

"The children," she lamented, "my sister Isabelle's children are left with no inheritance at all. And she was one of the wealthiest women in England." She sobbed and sobbed. "Richard, can't they come here to us?" Richard gave an unpleasant snarl.

"Fat chance! Can't see Edward allowing that!" And that was that.

Then, of course, all anyone could do was to wait for, litterally, the ax to fall. Anne became a shadow of her former self; mind, she'd never been robust to begin with. I kept well out of the way. Dark energy swirled around Middleham and I knew George's fate was sealed. I could hear Richard calling for me at times: 'Gaius!' I suppose he wanted to discuss the case; cats may be cruel but they don't drag out their kills for months – a few hours will do: it's a cat thing.
One day, I was lying in the main hall when Richard strode in. I got a dirty look.

"I've been looking for you," he said grumpily. "I thought you could make sense of what's going on." I hissed:

"I'm just a cat. What do you expect of me?" Richard picked me up and carried me under his arm as if I were a volume of the Encyclopedia Britannica.

"We have a visitor," was all he said. He went into his study and dumped me on the mantelpiece. I looked around. A fat sort of guy with a balding head sat mopping his face with a dirty handkerchief. He got to his feet when Richard came in and started 'my lord the duke'-ing but Richard cut him off quite brusquely.

"Never mind all that. I suppose you've come to tell me the deed is done." To me: "This is Sir Richard Catesby. You might say he is Edward's chief of staff." Prolonged silence. Richard waved his arms around impatiently, then shouted for a menial with refreshments. These arrived. Sir Catesby gulped down his share and held out his cup for seconds. Then he gulped and said:

"My Lord, I regret being the bearer of such grim news. Until the last, we waited … for the king to be merciful …" Richard snarled:

"Or change his mind? But there was never any hope of that surely." The handkerchief came out again and the moping renewed.

"Well, do you know, that on the day before … we had some hope that the king would change his mind. I had a long session with his Grace and he was very much of two minds about the affair. He then asked me to make out a warrant of reversal. You can imagine, my Lord, I got this done in the twinkle of an eye and brought the document to him. 'Leave it on my desk,' he said. 'I will consider it over lunch.' I can tell you I was hopeful. However, I had many other duties that day and when I finally returned to the king's study and looked for the warrant, it wasn't there. Which led me to think the king had signed it and sent it off."

There was a menacing silence. Sir Catesby wrung his hands. Richard shouted for some more wine. Obviously, Sir Catesby needed some Dutch courage.

"The next day," he continued, "I was appalled to learn that the execution had taken place and the Duke was dead." Another pause. "Although I was very afraid to do so, I went to the king and asked, as politely as I could, what had happened to the reversal document. The king looked at me in surprise. 'Why, I had been thinking of my conversation with my brother Richard, so I ordered the warrant be sent to the Tower immediately." He rummaged around in his papers. "I suppose we should be expecting George to blow in any time now." Richard gasped:

"He must have been having you on!" Sir Catesby answered, shaking his head sadly:

"My first thought, sir; I sat there stunned until he shouted at me.

'Well, now what?' I can tell you I shook and trembled but I drove myself on:

'Sire, I heard from Lord Brakenbury, your Majesty knows, the Lieutenant of the Tower …'

'I know, I know who Sir Brakenbury is,' he shouted. 'Will you get on with it?' So I did, all in a rush. 'Sire, the Duke of Clarence was executed this morning.' He got to his feet, came around the desk and leaned over the chair I was sitting in. I was terrified. He was so menacing. He said very slowly: 'I don't believe you. Get out of here, now, and don't let me see you again today!'" Since Sir Catesby's handkerchief was now dripping wet, Richard threw him one of his own.

"Go on."

"Well," Sir Catesby continued, "early next day I was called for. I can tell you I was shaking in my stockings when I went in. But the king seemed quite calm. He said:

'I think you'd better go off to Middleham and tell the Duke of Gloucester. Leave at once.' I tell you, I couldn't get away fast enough." Sir Catesby sniffed sadly. Richard's comment was:

"So here you are!"

"Indeed, my Lord Duke. I wish he had chosen someone else for this mission. On the other hand, I was glad to get away from the court and this strange tale. Who knows where it might lead…" Richard scratched his chin.

"An odd story, if I ever heard one." He looked daggers at Sir Catesby. "And you swear this is true?" He went over to his desk and picked up what I saw was a bible. "Swear," he barked, "swear on the Bible." Sir Catesby would have sworn on a stack of Bibles, the Koran or the Kamasutra if called upon to do so.

The meeting broke up with Sir Catesby being sent up to the second best guestroom for rest and recreation, I suppose, while Richard went to break the news to Anne who, true to form, wailed and sobbed for her niece and nephew.

Later that evening, Richard got a stiff drink and shut himself up in his bedroom, with me for company. While I found a suitable pillow to pummell until it was just right, Richard walked up and down the room. He muttered, almost to himself.

"The lot of us committed sins galore and the king could have made an attainder stick against anyone should he want to." I snickered:

"Edward prosecuted, didn't he? What were the accusations against George?"

Richard said through his teeth:

"Of being unnatural, lacking in loyalty and treason – all aggravated by being the King's brother."

"But nothing that could be proven? Like his plotting with Warwick?" Richard shook his head:

"Edward claimed the accusations were state secrets, thus could not be revealed." I smoothed my whiskers and had a bit of a stretch.

"If they had been, it would probably have meant bringing in others whom, at the moment, Edward wants to keep alive."

"Edward is a very stupid man, "I said. "And stupid men are very dangerous. They don't have imagination enough to make up accusations that could – but might not – be true." I rolled over. "Perhaps he'll go for you next." Richard took another turn.

"Truth to tell, members of the Commons don't care how many princes are executed or for what and the nobility have their own heads to think about. Anyhow, it's just as well we're all the way up here – in case Edward should get any more smart ideas." I said, in a meditative sort of way:

"I don't think you should forget, Richard, that once Edward dies, the only one standing between the Wydvilles and total power will be you, my friend."

2.3 High Crimes…

I fell fast asleep but some time during the night Richard woke me up.

"Cats don't sleep much at night, do they?" This was an odd question. I considered it.

"It all depends," I answered finally, "how much sleep they've had during the day." Richard didn't seem interested. Instead he said:

"I can't get George out of my mind, Gaius. I keep feeling there's something not quite right with all this."

"You mean, with Sir Catesby's story?" But Richard shook his head.

"No, I don't think Catesby has the intelligence or – as a matter of fact – the reason to make up such a preposterous story." We were quiet for a bit. Then I said:

"I think we need to consider the possibility, Richard, that George was murdered." Richard gasped:

"Have you taken leave of your senses, Gaius? Poor George had his head cut off by the public executioner at the Tower of London. How could that be classed as murder? Are you accusing the executioner? Don't be ridiculous!" Richard buried his face in his hands – he had a tendency to do so in times of stress. I sneered:

"Of course I don't consider the executioner a suspect," I answered smartly. "He has an unimpeachable alibi." Richard took his head out of his hands:

"How so?" he glared at me.

"Why," I said somewhat flippantly, "at the time of the murder he was in full view of a group of witnesses who will all swear he was cutting off George's head!" I laughed histerically at my own joke. Richard fumed:

"That, Gaius," he said bitterly, "was not funny." I wiped the smile off and said in a contrite way:

"Sorry, Richard, I just couldn't help it." We sat for a moment or two in silence. Then Richard went back to the beginning.

"Gaius, you say George may have been murdered. How did you get there?" I considered:

"It all depends on the reliability of Catesby, whom we both consider to be an unlikely suspect, and on the characteristics of your brother, Edward." Richard eyebrows shot up.

"We know my brother Edward is as unreliable as they come. But still … I just don't see …" I started to get impatient and waved my paws about.

"Richard, think. Edward draws up, signs and seals a warrant of execution against George and sends it to the Tower. The Lieutenant of the Tower, Sir Robert Brakenbury, looks at his execution agenda and slots poor George in for Thursday next, say. This fact is not under dispute. We know Edward signed the warrant and, if you ask Sir Robert, he will confirm it and show you all his logs and entries.

"What is in dispute is: Edward tells Sir Catesby he is considering changing his mind; he has Sir Catesby draw up a warrant of reversal, cancelling, so to speak, the execution. If we take Sir Catesby at his word and the second warrant really does – or did – exist, and Edward really was going to pardon George, what happened to this second warrant?" Richard looked bewildered:

"How should I know?" I hissed in irritation.

"Really, Richard, sometimes you're such a moron. If I tell you George was murdered, how do you think it was done?" Now it was Richard's turn to become irritatted.

"Gaius, for the umpteenth time, George was beheaded at the Tower." I lifted a paw, one claw extended.

"No, Richard. George died because the warrant of reversal did not reach the Tower." Richard scratched his head. After a bit, he said:

"Are you telling me that George didn't die because his head was cut off but because the second warrant did not exist or got lost?" He scratched his chin. "So the murder weapon was not the executioner's ax but the warrant of reverasal."

"That's my boy," I said, pleased. "Always assuming, of course, that Sir Catesby and Edward aren't lying about the second warrant." Richard shook his head.

"If Edward wanted George dead, there was no one to stop him." We looked at each other.

"Let's recapitulate," I said, holding up my left paw so I could tick off, so to speak, the relevant points:

"Your brother George was incarcerated in the Tower by order of your brother Edward, at the instigation, you claim, of Ma Wydville. Is that correct?" Richard made a face at me.

"Of course it is, we can all agree on that."

"George is prosecuted in the Commons, with Edward as prosecutor. The Commons issue a warrant of attainder against him. Now, according to Sir Catesby, at the last moment Edward changed his mind about George and another warrant was issued to cancel and supercede the first, setting George free. Are you with me?" Richard stopped pacing and sat down.

"Yes, yes. When are you going to tell me something I don't know?" I didn't deign to answer but went on:

"Now, when a warrant of execution is made out, it is sent to the Tower, right?" I asked.

"Yes, yes." Richard was getting exasperated

"And then the person is executed."

"Well, usually first thing next morning."

"I see. So the condemned man can get a good night's sleep." I sniffed.

"Gaius, don't try to be funny."

"Richard, I am not trying to be funny. Let us say that the warrant of execution was sent to the Tower on a certain day so George's execution would take place the next morning."

"And?"

"The afternoon before Edward has second thoughts, has Catesby make out the warrant of reversal which, unfortunately, never reaches the Tower – although Edward firmly believes it was sent."

"I'll be damned. I'll be damned. So what happened to it?"

"Ah," I said, "that's the six million shilling question: perhaps Edward forgot about it. Or," I sat up straight and tucked my tail neatly around my back paws, "it was intercepted to make sure it did not reach the Tower." Richard went back to pacing. I continued: "Perhaps Sir Robert surpressed it for reasons of his own." Richard snarled:

"Rubbish. Sir Robert is an honest man. And why should he want George dead, anyway? Can't see it would do him any good." I shrugged:

"If you say so." Richard paced some more and I continued: "now: when looking for a murderer, there are three facts to consider: *motive, means* and *opportunity* or, to put it another way, *why, how* and *when.* A suspect, he – or she – must meet these criteria."

Richard looked rather blank so I continued with my lesson: "Let's take a few examples, shall we? The executioner: he had the means (the ax) and opportunity (he was there) but no motive. Sir Robert had opportunity (he was there) no means (the ax), and, as far as we know, no motive." Richard seemed more and more confused. I went on. "However, we can discard those two because we agree that the murder was not committed by the blow of an ax but by the suppression of a document." I stopped, took a deep breath and threw myself into it: "Now, let's look at you, Richard." Richard sat up and took notice.

"What do you mean, me? I wasn't even there." He frowned. I waved my paw at him.

"My dear fellow, in any case of suspicious death, one always looks at the family first. About 95% of victims are murdered by someone they know. We've looked at Edward and have excluded him, for now. But did you have a motive?"

"For wanting George dead? Give me one."

"Perhaps," I said, "if George had survived, you would have been passed over as Lord Protector – he, after all, is the senior Plantagenet once Edward is gone." Richard ground his teeth.

"Gaius, I don't know why I put up with you. Besides the fact that I have no desire of becoming Lord Protector, Edward would never have trusted George that far. They might have kissed and made up but even you should be able to see that all would never be well between them." There was no arguing with that. I continued:

"I take it there was no chance of your getting some of George's estate since Anne, your wife, was George's wife's sister?" But Richard shook his head.

"No, Gaius; we've already discussed this. An attainder results in the person concerned having his entire estate which, in George's case, was substantial, forfeit to the Crown. Should George be pardoned and released, he would, of course, get everything back." I chewed on the claws on my left paw.

"So that makes you a bit of a washout as a suspect," I said. "Your motive is flimsy at best, although, let us not forget, if Edward dies soonish – as may well be the case – and you become Lord Protector, you take possession of the crown's goods and chattels. As we are looking at a warrant that, if it ever existed, has disappeared, perhaps you have an agent in London who made it disappear?" Richard barked which gave me quite a shock until I realized it was a bitter laugh.

"If you think Ma Wydville would ever have left any of my agents anywhere near Edward's official correspondence, you are not as smart as you think you are." I had to agree. I couldn't see Ma Wydville allowing anyone a free run of the royal apartments.

"Now, if we agree I had no motive, means or opportunity," he continued, "that seems to leave us with only one suspect." I raised my eyebrows:

"And that is?"

"The Wydville faction." Now it was Richard's turn to count on his fingers. "Motive: one less senior Plantagenet; or pure and simple greed for the Clarence estate. Opportunity: don't make me laugh. Means: plenty of cash, enough to bribe a hundred chamberlains, heralds and so on."

Well, Richard was turning into quite a detective. And, really, we were otherwise all out of suspects. The Wydvilles were the only game in town. I mussed:

"As George was never released, the crown gets his estate and when Edward dies it all goes to his son, little Edward, your oh so sweet nephew." Richard glared:

"You're not going to suggest that the kid Edward, who is anyway cooped up in a damp castle at Ludlow on the Welsh border, planned and carried out the murder of his uncle?" I held up my paws.

"No," I answered, "I do not. However, Edward has an extended family and, during Edward's minority, who knows into what pockets George's estate will wander? Anxious and willing pockets are not in short supply." Richard sat up and slammed his hands into the headboard of his bed.

"Those damned Wydvilles. They will swallow up the whole kingdom before they're done. Greed I know but these lowborn nobodies have given the word a whole new meaning." And dimension, thinks I.

"But our whole case rests," I reminded him, "on a warrant of reversal being drawn up and willfully suppressed. Perhaps the whole incident can be blamed on laziness or apathy of the civil service; we all know what they are like."

"Perhaps," said Richard, "it was just plain evil and malice and these need no reason." But I shook my head.

"You're wrong, Richard. Everyone talks of evil as a stand alone but there is always a motive behind it. Perhaps you don't like your neighbour's dog or God told you to destroy all redheads, whatever, so you (metaphorically speaking) kill.

"In this case, the motive must have been strong: surpressing the second warrant was taking a terrible chance. Had it gone wrong, George would still be around with his property, a new royal wife, his place in the succession and so on. So far the murderer's luck has held. Now that George is dead, the whole thing will be forgotten." I lay on my side and had a good stretch, which always helps my thinking process. "There should be a chain of evidence but I don't think how we can find it," was my final comment. Richard, who had thrown himself down on the bed, half rose up:

"Really, Gaius, sometimes I don't know what you're on about. What do you mean – chain of evidence? What kind of chain is that?"

"Richard," I said, "a chain has a first link, a second and so on to the last link. Metaphorically, an event is made up of actions, one tied to the next, just like a chain. So let's see where this chain takes us." I continued hurriedly as I saw Richard about to reach for his shoe. "The last link was the beheading of George."

"Don't," said Richard through barred teeth, "talk about it as if you were buying a bunch of carrots."

"Ok, ok, keep your shirt on! The next link is the headsman being told to polish his ax. Probably by Sir Robert."

"Who," mussed Richard, "is a man of honour." Well, I had my doubts but wasn't about to get into that again. I continued:

"Sir Robert would have received the official warrant of execution directly from the king's herald or one of the Tower guards. So the links between the warrant of execution from Palace to Tower are clear. The second warrant has a link from Catesby to the King and then on to Sir Robert at the Tower. But there is no proof that the warrant went from the palace to the Tower. So it was either destroyed within palace or was intercepted before reaching Sir Robert at the Tower." Richard twiddled his thumbs and I continued: "I guess we'll never know. We can't question the king or the Wydvilles."

"As for the heralds, there are so many of them one wouldn't know where to begin," added Richard. "So, we're stumped."

"Actually," I concluded, "my guess is that the second warrant never left the king's desk." We were both silent and thoughtful. "So," I went on, "we come to outcome or you could say result. What was the outcome of George's death? His property goes to the crown." Richard shrugged.

"As far as I can see, no one benefitted from George's death. He had no power. He had no credibility. His wife was dead as was his father in law, Warwick, the king maker." He glared at me. "All this speculation is not getting us anywhere." I had to agree.

"It can't be about the succession, seeing Edward has two healthy boys who would have to be eliminated before Clarence could become king." Richard nodded. I went on. "Say you wanted to become king; a lot of people would have to disappear." I went on. "Clarence well, he's gone. Then Edward, prince of Wales, Richard, duke of York, followed by George's son, Edward." We sat silently for a while. Then I said:

"Another way to look at it, Richard, is that someone is getting rid of the old royal line. George is gone. Edward will not last too long. You are now the only obstacle between the Wydvilles and full power and control over England. If you were to die, why, it would all be plain sailing. Edward is a minor, and for years a Lord Protector will hold power." Richard said thoughtfully:

"And if I were named Lord Protector..." I could see his mind working.

"If I were you," I cautioned, "I would be extremely careful not to end up like poor George. And hope Edward dies before Ma W can get back to her spells and cauldrons. The matter of the letter G seems to have been entirely forgotten although it's still got legs. It may well be used next."

"Enough!" shouted Richard and throw a cushion at me – a wasted effort. But he had really and truly had enough. He crawled under the covers fully clothed, down to his boots. I did that special cat stretch – front and back paws as far as they could go in opposite directions, curved spine, trying to touch my head with my tail.

"Richard, how about a tummy rub? It would feel really good!" A snarl came from the bed:

"Have you gone out of your mind?" Rats. I could have done with a tummy rub.

I was just dropping off when:

"Gaius…" I opened half an eye.

"Yeah?"

"We've forgotten someone!"

"Victim or suspect. I can't stand the suspense. Do tell, Richard."

"Henry Tudor."

"You think Henry Tudor came over from Brittany, marched into your brother Edward's study, picked up the second warrant and took it back to Brittany, making sure poor George got beheaded?" Silence. Then:

"Nooo. I just don't think we should forget about him."

"Right. When Edward's dead, his two kids are dead, George's kid is dead and you're dead and Eddie is dead, then we can start worrying about Henry." Silence. Over and out.

Later, thinking this matter over, I decided that, whether George's death had been *de facto* or *de jure*, it was the event that precipitated all that followed. Had George been around, everything would have turned out differently. On the other hand, Richard needed to watch his back. It might well be his turn next. It seemed to me that someone wanted power very badly and Richard was the last man standing.

As I was falling asleep that night a thought took hold of my brain and wouldn't let go. Impeachment. Why was I thinking of impeachment? That was something the Americans upper crust did when they didn't like the guy the people had elected. Could it be that Edward IV had commited an impeachable offence? I ruminated. After all, George was a royal Duke and offing one of those shouldn't be just another routine task before lunch. one might easily run out of royal dukes after just a few.

My eyes were closing and the thought ran away.

3

Edward IV

3.1 Off to London

One day in early spring, I was shaken awake by Richard, already fully dressed It was still dark outside. I shook my head.

"What are you doing here? Weren't you supposed to be fighting the Scots? Or have you killed them all?"

"No time for your funny bits," came the answer. "The king is dying, which is bad news for me as I don't feel competent or prepared to take on all those Wydvilles. But needs must when the devil drives." I stretched. The news that Edward IV was not expected to survive didn't really come as much as a surprise, given that the national health care then was not much better than it is now. I looked at Richard:

"So Edward is off, is he? But what's that to me? You can tell me all about it when you get back," and I turned my back to him. But though there might not be many broken hearts in Middleham, Richard said we must all go to London for the happy event – me included. Richard sneered:

"You're so clever with all your ideas of means and motives and chains and such. You can continue accumulating what was it you called it – facts." And clues. Oh, well. If I must, I must.

Eddie was very excited since he had never been out of Yorkshire before. We were all bundled into carriages or carts, wagons following with the Gloucesters' paraphernalia including servants and so on. Of course Eddie had to be bundled in with me. I curled up immediately, hoping that the little blighter would leave me alone. Some hope! He hung out of the window, anxious not to miss any of the great sights.

"This is real cool, Gaius," he said as we jostled along.

"Yeah," says I, "just like a roller coaster." He looked at me enquiringly.

"What's a roller coaster?" I closed my eyes firmly. Some things can't be explained. But there was no way of shutting him up; all the way to London he was ecstatic.

"Look, Gaius, a cow! Do look, Gaius, I think that's a war horse. Oh, see all those cute lambs! A castle, castle! Who do you think it belongs to?" I shut my eyes. But the torrent continued. I never knew a kid with such a thirst for information. Finally we arrived in London. Eddie pointed at every bridge we passed, crying out:

"Gaius, is that London bridge? And where is the Tower? Gaius, show me the Tower!" The less you know about the Tower, my lad, the better for you.

However, all bad things come to an end as the man says and eventually we arrived at Baynard's castle, where the happy mother of Edward and Richard was waiting for us. She was covered in black; considering how people died in her family, it mustn't have seemed worthwhile to buy anything else. She had her grandchildren – George's children, another Edward and a girl, Margaret. This Edward looked a bit dazed and gave the impression he wasn't all there, so to speak. The girl looked more alert. I tried not to look at them knowing how their lives would end[x].

The news was that Edward was still hanging on to life so Richard decided we should rest up before going to the palace.

3.2 A Good Day's Work

So the next day we all went to Westminster and joined the throng of mourners. The whole court was there. The king was still alive. There was no stilted conversation; it seemed no one was talking to anyone else. I found a mantlepiece and lay there on my side, eyes half shut, tail swinging softly. And so the long morning wore on until one of the king's equerries entered – our old friend Sir William Catesby – bowed to the Queen:

"Madam, the king is asking for your presence and of these gentlemen." The Queen, addressing all her best friends, said:

"Gentlemen, shall we?" She lead the way, the rest following with little enthusiasm. The Duchess of York, Anne and all the children stayed behind. I crept in last and slipped beneath a heavy sideboard, lying quietly in the shadows.

Edward IV was installed on his throne, supported by pillows with screens around him to keep off the draft. Everyone was there: the Queen, Lords Rivers, Grey and Dorset, the Duke of Buckingham, Lord Hastings and so on. King Edward sighed, and looked at the assembly wistfully. He said:

"I hear you have buried your quarrels and have reached a truly noble and lasting agreement. I rejoice and now feel I am ready to meet my Redeemer who, I believe, will be calling me into His presence soon. My soul is at peace and ready for its last great journey." Kings are always optimistic of where they are going after death. He went on:

"Hastings and Rivers, let bygones be bygones. Forget the past. And build a prosperous and happy future." Hastings bowed low and said:

"So I so do swear!" He held out his hand to Lord Rivers. That left Rivers with no way out – should he have contemplated one – and the two shook hands. Lord Grey was next:

"Upon my soul, I do swear the like!" Edward waggled his finger at them in a playful manner:

"Now, see you hold to your sworn oaths for He, the supreme Being, will surely look into your souls, detect any falsehood and decree one of you to be the other's end." I struggled a bit with this sentence and decided it meant that one would kill the other. But then, if oathbreakers faced instant death on a regular basis, humanity would have ceased to exist long ago. Dream on, Edward.

Having settled this to his satisfaction, Edward turned towards his wife, while the new sworn friends glared at each other. The King said:

"Madam, you are not exempt from taking part in the breaches that have come between your kin and the nobility." Oh, oh, that must have grated. "Nor you, my son Grey or, for that matter, you, my dear

Duke of Buckingham." Buckingham opened his mouth to protest his eternal love, I suppose, but the King silenced him. "Wife, love Lord Hastings; let him kiss your hand and do so in friendship and openness." Elizabeth held out her hand limply and said sweetly.

"My Lord Hastings, I have quite forgotten our former differences, and I do swear with an open heart for myself and mine." Hastings bowed low and kissed her hand.

"Whatever may have caused our disagreements," he said, "I assure you I can no longer remember how they came about." I sighed. Hypocrisy always makes me nauseous. Easy to forget, indeed, since the king no longer needed a pimp. With these two sorted, Edward went down his little list:

"Now, son Grey, do you embrace Lord Hastings and let bonds of friendship tie you forever."

"For my part, this oath shall be inviolable," volunteered Hastings; like Buckingham, he seemed to have been primed and was all candour. Grey's contribution was:

"And so do I, in all solemnity, swear." More and more pleased with himself, Edward turned to Buckingham:

"Princely Buckingham," that should have stung too; no one else had been called princely. "Take my wife and her family to your heart and make me blessed seeing you all united in peace and love." Buckingham turned on a huge smile and faced the queen, falling on his knee before her:

"Madam, should I have shown the slightest enmity towards you or yours, may God punish me by turning to hate the love of those dearest to me." Edward sank back into pillows with a sigh of contentment:

"My good Buckingham, your words are as a balm on my heart. All I now wish for is to see my dearest brother, Richard. Sir William," turning to Catesby, "where is the Duke of Gloucester, my beloved brother." Well, Richard had been hanging back and was lost in the shadows of the huge hall. Catesby ran up to him and he reluctantly stepped forward and bowed to his brother.

"My king, it gladens my heart to see you in such good spirits." Edward smiled indulgently, still floating on his little pink cloud, quite divorced from the real world around him and totally oblivious to the negative energy floating around caused by hate, envy, greed and ambition. To my surprise, Richard's energy level was so negative it was off the charts. The king said genially:

"We have spent a most happy hour, dear brother, in making friends of enemies and turning hate into love. I am content now that my kingdom, my England, will remain a peaceful realm once I am gone." The old hypocrite. But then, one must make allowances for the terminally ill. Richard gave a rather tight smile:

"That has indeed been a labour of love, my Lord, for what reasons could there be for hate among those of us present here? What need for acrimony, jealousy or vindictiveness? I shall gladly repeat again what I have already said," and he turned towards the Wydvilles: "Madam, I beg there may be peace between us. You may rest assured I shall always at your service. As for Lords Rivers, Dorset and Grey, I hereby swear I have ever been their friend and will continue to be so. In fact, I swear that I have never been at odds with any of those present in this chamber nor am I at odds with any Englishman, be he ne'er so humble. Come, we are all brothers in Christ."

"Oh, bravo, dearest Richard," enthused the king. But Richard's face did not radiate any sweetness and light – I crept further into the shadows. When there's trouble afoot, household pets should keep out of the way as they are likely the first to be kicked.

Richard now said in a low dangerous voice.

"Indeed, I offer friendship and love to all those here; but that is a mockery, is it not, my brother? For where is my other brother, George, Duke of Clarence? How can there be peace and love when brother slays brother? Fratricide! The first murder in the Holy Book! And you, my brother Edward, ordered the death of your brother, George!" There was a common gasp. What, had poor George been quite forgotten? OK, his demise may have been a few years ago but, as the Americans say, there is no statute of limitation on murder. Richard continued, brows lowered. "I feel his corpse defiled by the callousness and hypocrisy I see around me." King Edward half rose from his throne:

"My dear brother Richard, George was a traitor to the realm. His death was ordered by Parliament!" Richard sneered:

"Oh, really, Edward, it was all the doing of Parliament! When have you ever listened to Parliament? It just did what you ordered it to do.

George was not their brother so why should they care? You ordered his death. You signed his death warrant!" Edward's face twisted:

"It was not my fault, Richard. It was not. Yes, I confess to signing the death warrant, but then I reversed it!" wailed the king, half rising. "It is hardly my fault if the second warrant went astray!"

"Indeed, brother," sneered Richard, "but at the end of the day George died on your say so and on your watch. No matter how often you may blame others – the herald fell off his horse, the constable of the Tower was at a party – the mark of Cain, the blood of a brother, is on your head and will be there when you meet your Maker."

The King held out his arms and started to collapse, gasping for breath, then clasping his hands to his left breast.

"He was a traitor," the king gasped. "Parliament ordered his execution."

"Really," answered, Richard, "or did you feel threatened by his attempt to marry into European royalty! And if he had, his power would have been great!" The King rose to his feet, then fell forward, gasping for breath and reaching out. Heart attack, thinks I. Edward IV was as usual taking the easy way out. The Queen, aided by Lord Hastings, helped him from the throne, taking him, I suppose, to his bedroom; most of the Wydvilles trailed along.

Buckingham turned to Richard, looking truly aghast.

"This is awful, my Lord Gloucester. He is your brother, he is your king. And to accuse him thus as he lies dying. And he did try to stop the execution, Richard, he really did!"

"Is that so!" Richard answered grimly. "Did the order of reversal actually exist? And if it did, where did it get to?" He turned and pointed at Buckingham. "Do you know?"

"Me?" cried Buckingham his eyes as big as saucers, "why, no one at court has spoken to me for ever so long."

"I have kept well away," replied Richard glumly. "I don't care if he is dying; the execution of a brother I cannot forgive. Whatever George's faults, they were no worse than Edward's, mine, your's or anyone else's." He marched out, and I slipped after him, down to the Thames and on to a waiting barge.

3.3 A king Bows Out

Next day, the whole party at Barnyard's embarked on a waiting barge and set off. Arriving at the Palace, everyone else was gathered in the king's bedroom so in our party went. I crept in silently behind them and jumped up on a table standing against a far wall, curling up behind a tasteful floral arrangement. The Wydville family were there en masse, plus Buckingham, Hastings, Stanley and other luminaries of the court.

The king's end was near. He lay sunk in pillows, eyes unfocused, mouth open. Suddenly he seemed to rally, managed to half sit up and, with his last breath and in his last lucid moment, cried out:

"Richard! My true brother Richard. Hear you all – Catesby, take this down as my last will and testament. I name my brother Richard Lord Protector of the realm once I am gone." He swept his dying glance around the room, croacking out: "You all stand witness. Richard of Gloucester will be Lord Protector until my son comes of age." Edward IV sank back on to his pillows and died, leaving the entire mess behind. Mind you, given who he was and how he had lived his life, it was well within his modus operandi.

It's not an overstatement to say that everyone looked shocked. After the mayhem of the day before between Richard and Edward, this was the last the Wydvilles expected. Had Edward himself forgotten all about it or did he, at the time of his death, acknowledge that Richard was his one true friend? Did Edward acknoledge the awfulness of his sin in slaying his brother?

3.4 Another High Crime?

It was time to get dressed for the wake, I presume, so leaving Elisabeth Wydville to wail and tear her hair and garments surrounded by her family, the Barnyard party returned to its barge and up the river it went. Back in Richard's room, I lay on my favourite pillow while Richard got into his mourning togs. Lots of black, except for gems gleaming here and there. People in those days were as vain as peacocks. Richard looked at me sort of sideways and said, sneeringly:

"I suppose you are going to tell me that my brother Edward was murdered, too. What is it you call it? You identify motive, means and opportunity, a chain of events and then just pop the guy in the Tower." He laughed. I looked at him through slit eyes. Don't meddle with cats, it will never do you any good. I said:

"Evidence, Richard. All this is called evidence and can be presented in a court of law although I'm sure you're not familiar with any such institution, that is, a proper one." I didn't give him a chance to protest but carried on: "Well, there is a good chance your brother was indeed murdered and he certainly deserved to be. But, if he was, I must say the means where totally unorthodox and the outcome uncertain to say the least." He looked at me, frowning:

"What do you mean?"

"Well," I said, stretching myself and curling up in a more comfortable position. "Motive: I can't say for sure what the motive was because, as far as I can see, it was in almost everyone's interest to keep Edward alive as long as possible. Except..."

"Except for what?" flashed Richard.

"Except," I said sweetly, "for you. You are the only one with a motive for wanting your brother dead as soon as possible, his heir as young as possible so that you, as Lord Protector, would have complete control of the realm."

"I don't believe what I'm hearing," came the incredulous answer.

"Oh, yes, Richard," I said calmly, "you and you alone had a motive for wishing your brother dead. So. Motive: Richard of Gloucester: absolute power over the realm. Means: well, easy. You brought on Edward's final stroke when you accused him of George's murder. You were harsh and brutal and Edward couldn't take it. After that, it was just a question of waiting. Opportunity: when Edward was at his most vulnerable, in the middle of spreading eternal peace and love among his nearest and dearest." Richard gritted his teeth:

"Cat, I am going to wring your neck."

"That," I answered calmly, "would be very easy for I am a small and frail animal. But it would solve nothing. To continue. There is one problem: whoever killed the king also killed George and as we have already discussed, in the case of George you had neither the means nor the opportunity. Nor do I believe you could have engineered the chain of events linking Clarence's to Edward's deaths."

"So, according to you," shouted Richard, "Someone killed both my brothers."

"Oh," I waved a languid paw, "I have no doubt of that in the case of poor George. However, in the case of Edward, it all becomes more difficult. Our perpretators of choice – the Wydvilles – stand to gain nothing and to lose much since you are Lord Protector for the next six years or so. You may have been manipulated by someone much cleverer than you, who knew you well enough to predict that, when Edward was on his deathbed, you would bring up the matter of George. Not all that hard, since you've been yammering about poor George all over the place since his arrest and execution. You may have been played upon, my dear Gloucester, like a flute."

"Do you really think I am that easy to read? That I am so shallow people know what I think and how I react in a given situation?" There was a menace in Richard voice. But, me, what do I care.

"I am afraid, Richard, that I do."

"And who do you then think is this mastermind?" I didn't feel like answering this because Richard would certainly not like it. But then. Some rain in each life must fall.

"Well," I said quietly. "There's the Duke of Buckingham. With you in control, he has a better chance of getting his estates back. " Richard sneered as I knew he would.

"You think I can't outsmart Buckingham? Then I must really be a basket case." I continued:

"Let's say that he had help or was managed by an outside agency."

"Such as?" I hemmed and hawed. Then took the plunge.

"Margaret Beaufort. Think, Richard, should Edward die after his son reaches his majority, there's no hope in hell Henry Tudor will ever be king. On the other hand, someone like the Lord Protector might be easier to manage."

"Ha! Buckingham and Margaret Beaufort, indeed!" Richard got up in a fury and slammed out of the room. Poor Richard. He meant well and that in the end may have led to his downfall. Well, it's only a theory. But I thought it sounded good. Devil to prove in court, of course.

The thought of impeachment raced through once more after I had curled up on my favourite pillow. If, as I had said to Richard, Edward IV was offed, that would certainly be a high crime, more so than in the case of poor George. Really, it seemed that the Plantagenets were falling like flies. Only one left at the moment – Richard.

4

The Lord Protector

4.1 Off with the old and on with the new

Back at the Westminster, there were bleeding hearts aplenty. The Duchess of York wept for her husband and sons. Clarence children sat next to their grandmother with frightened faces. Even Edward of Middleham had finally nothing to say. He sat next to his mother and, just to be nice, I joined them.

Queen Elisabeth's laments were the loudest of all; she mourned her husband but most of all she feared for her future. Richard mourned for George and perhaps a bit for Edward, not Edward the king who was no great loss, but for the Edward of their shared childhood, youth and comradeship-in-arms.

The start of a new reign. The old king was dead. And with a child as heir, what would the harvest be? Boy kings have a habit of getting lost in the shuffle for power and at that moment England seemed to be up for grabs. The only positive point was that the two rival factions – the traditional hereditary aristocracy, represented by Richard, Buckingham, Derby, Hastings and so on –and the Wydvilles, nobodies from nowhere who, by a role of the die or, if you prefer, a fluke of luck, had ascended to unbelievable heights; the two sides would keep each other in check, at least for a time.

Queen Elizabeth was surrounded by her sons, Lords Dorset and Grey, her brother, Lord Rivers, as well as by Richard of York, the younger of her sons with Edward and I don't know how many daughters. She wept and wept. Her attire was all anyhow and her hair needed a good shampoo and a brush but I suppose there are times when such things are not a woman's highest priority. In an attempt to console her, or at least stem the flow of tears, her older sons knelt by her and whispered what I took to be words of consolation. But then the Queen lifted her face from her sodden handkerchief and cried out:

"Oh, now my husband is gone and what will become of me and my children? And who can dry my tears or stop me tormenting myself with visions of the future? How can we continue to live when he, who was our guardian and protector, is gone? Oh, that I could have gone with him; but, as I cannot, let me weep." Sounded good, no doubt, and to be sure Elisabeth had reason to shed tears. I didn't think much of her menfolk. Earl Rivers cleared his throat.

"My sister, grieve if you must and so you should but do not forget your son, the young prince, who is now king. He shall be the comfort of your life. Bury your sorrows for the Edward who has gone to his grave and sow your joys in the Edward who shall grow and thrive." Elisabeth shook here head in despair.

"Oh, my brother, if only I had your confidence. But Richard is Lord Protector and he loves me not." That may be true, lady, but you don't love him either so you have no reason to complain.

It was at this moment that Richard entered, with the Duke of Buckingham, Lord Hastings and Sir Richard Ratcliffe, a compère of Richard's I had not yet met. I took a look. He had a shifty way about him. But then so had Buckingham. In fact, except for Richard, I wouldn't have trusted any of them further than I could throw a stick. Hastings, now, I was not so sure of Hastings. Anyone who has been in the Tower and gotten out alive was either really innocent or incredibly guilty. Richard looked around at the mournful assembly.

"This is a sad day for us all. In our different capacities, we have all lost someone dear to us. A husband, father and brother-in-law," with a nod to Elizabeth and her crew, "two sons," looking at his mother, "and of course George's children who have lost their father and now their uncle." Buckingham injected his own little homily, a sad smile on his pudgy face. The king of hypocrites.

"It was so fortunate that our dearly beloved King, now departed, managed to bring us all together in friendship and love, so that in friendship and love we may begin a new reign, a reign of peace, cooperation and prosperity for all Englishmen." Everyone looked duly solemn. Richard broke in before Buckingham got too maudlin':

"You all know my beloved brother named me Lord Protector while the new king is in his minority." No congratulations from anyone, but Hastings, Buckingham and Ratcliffe all looked pleased. Elizabeth sighed:

"It seems so, indeed, my Lord." The Duchess of York added:

"May God bless you, my son, and put mercy in your breast, so you may carry out this most important office with love, charity, obedience and a sense of true duty." Richard bent down and kissed her.

"My dear mother, you know that it is my wish to serve. I am here to carry out Edward's wishes." He patted her hand. "So," he continued, "I would like to call a first meeting of the new Council of State soonest, to be held in the great hall of the Tower. Madame," he bowed to his mother, "and you, Madam," to Elizabeth, "be of good heart. If we have had sorrow in the past, let us make sure the future will bring nothing but joy."

The late unlamented King Edward was buried at Windsor Castle's, St George's Chapel, on 9 April (where he would later be joined by Ma Wydville). So, as a last insult, Edward made the whole court trog off to Windsor during a cold week in April. I elected to stay behind. Richard was insisting that I come, too, but this time I really preferred to stay with Eddie. Richard said:

"Gaius, it will be an education; burying the king will be a splendid affair. The bishops and priests will wear their finest vestments, all the church bells will toll mournfully and the choir will sing hymns to the dead and the resurrection. When will you have the chance to see a king buried?" But I was adamant.

"Richard, cats don't do funerals, or weddings either. Cats are born and live in the moment. As for education, cats use empiricism (based on experience) or atavism (genetic knowledge handed down from cat to cat over the generations). When we die, we return to the soil and resume our role in the natural cycle." I stretched out and laid my head on my paw. "I've told my flatmate that, when I die, she is just throw me out of the window. But she insists on a full cremation."

Richard left in as many coats as he had before I could develop on my theme. I was going to say that cats don't marry because to be stuck with the same cat, even for our short life span of 15 years, would be too boring.

"What does a bishop look like?" asked Eddie. I sighed.

"There was one at your christening," was my parry. That shut Eddie up but not for long.

"But I can't remember," he said at last. I covered my ears with my paws and went to sleep.

4.2 The Council meeting

After that, the business of the new reign could begin in earnest and the Council, consisting of Richard, Earl Rivers, Lord Grey, the Duke of Buckingham, Lord Hastings and Sir Ratcliffe duly forgathered in the great hall at the Tower, with Richard as, in the modern sense, chairman, at the head of the oblong and ancient oak table with the others scattered around as they liked. I was there, too; Richard had brought me along, mostly to annoy the others. He began:

"Dear friends, the order of the day is of course the coronation of the new king, Edward V." Buckingham cleared his throat.

"Indeed, and I think it advisable that the young Prince be brought at once to London accompanied by a small train of nobles and retainers." Earl Rivers frowned:

"A small train, my Lord Duke. Why should that be? I would think all the foremost nobles of England would wish to accompany the Prince on his journey to his capital." Buckingham smiled sweetly.

"You are so right, Earl Rivers, as you always are. However, it would be quite impossible to include them all, and those left out might feel excluded, passed over, or what you will, and become jealous and malicious. A small train of immediate family and members of the very highest nobility would avoid creating unrest and difficulties while the government is still unsecured." Richard nodded in agreement:

"I agree with Lord Buckingham. At this state in our affairs, many a lord may think himself free to follow his own inclinations, whatever these may be, and that we must prevent at all costs. I for one declare myself firm and true to the compact the late king made between us." Albeit reluctantly, Earl Rivers agreed:

"The case is well put by both the Lord Protector and the Duke of Buckingham; a small train will also move faster so the new king reaches London all the sooner. And I think I also speak for my sister, the Queen." He got a frigid look from Richard.

"Although I have great respect for your sister, the dowager queen, please remember that she is not a member of this Council. We will always wish for her support but do not need her approval." Rivers went red. The others nodded. Richard went on:

"So it is decided. Earl Rivers, you will be lead the prince's escort and you, Lord Hastings, will accompany him. Choose whomsoever you wish to complete the party. I will personally select 100 top archers and swordsmen to protect the prince and his train." Scrapping and bowing, everyone left except Richard and Buckingham. As soon as the door closed, Buckingham turned to Richard and said nervously:

"You cannot be serious, my friend. You are delivering the prince to the Wydvilles and what will be the outcome of that? You and I should certainly not stay at home." Richard threw his arm through Buckingham's.

"My dear cousin," he said soothingly, "you are not thinking straight. The Wydvilles may think they are in control because they hold the prince. But I am Lord Protector, my friend, and at the moment that counts for everything; I hold London and the Tower and that means I hold England. And don't forget: the soldiers who will protect the prince on this journey will be loyal to me and their commander, Sir James Tyrell, is my man.

"But I'll think of what you've said and consider whether it would be wise to meet the royal party at the halfway mark." So we all left, Buckingham going whether it was he hung out and Richard and I got into the barge to take us up the Thames to Barnyard's castle.

"Well, smarty-pants," said Richard with derision once we were in his bedroom, "and what do you make of all that?" I stretched and replied:

"*Pace* the Arabs[3]: *the enemy of my enemy is not necessarily my friend although we may travel together part of the way.*" This time the pillow hit me and I fell off my perch on the back of a upholstered chair. Tail in air and head held high, I walked out of the room with dignity.

---

[3]   Originally:: "The enemy of my enemy is my friend."

5

Edward V

5.1 From Ludlow to London

The Lord Protector, a.k.a., Richard of Gloucester, moved into Westminister with wife and son, cat, kit and caboodle and took over the chambers where his dead brother had administered (when not otherwise engaged in shagging the local girls, hunting, stuffing himself and drinking) his realm. Richard, on the contrary, didn't eat much, shagging the ladies was not his thing, as for hunting that was soo not Richard, although he liked a gentle ride now and then.

Instead, he was always at it with bits of paper, arguing with his appointments secretary over the precedence of visiting foreign ambassadors, looking into the kingdom's finances with diverse very nervous accountants; the finances were a right mess as a result of the Edward's tolerance of the Wydvilles' rapaciousness, to say nothing of his own wasteful lifestyle.

Richard's secretaries and clerks rushed in and out of his study either bringing something or to draft something. I was lying lazily on the desk watching the minions scampering to and through in a whirl of activity, when the Duke of Buckingham came in, completely unannounced. He went round the desk and whispered in Richard's ear. Richard flew out of his chair, almost knocking my Lord Duke off his feet, his face flaming red.

"You what?" he shouted. Buckingham straightened himself up, looking mifted.

"I just told you. I have brought the young prince to London."

"You? And when was this decided? I seem to remember we discussed it in council and the final decision was taken by myself as Lord Protector that Lord Rivers should lead the entourage!" Buckingham straightened his collar.

"Come off it, Richard. We are in this together, you and I, why, we talked the whole thing through after the council meeting." Richard stamped his foot:

"Oh, we did, did we? How come I don't recall the conversation coming to this particular conclusion? You said we shouldn't stay at home and I told you I would think about it." Buckingham threw up his hands in exasperation.

"Yes, and when did you ever get back to me?" Richard ground his teeth.

"And silence means consent, I take it? And where then are Earl Rivers and Lord Grey plus Sir Vaughn who were given the task of accompanying the prince to London?" Buckingham examined his nails.

"In Pomfret Castle."

"I see," Richard's voice was dangerous, "in Pomfret Castle. And why are they in Pomfret castle? Did they decide to break their journey for a little holiday?"

"Of course not. I had them arrested."

"I see. And on whose orders, may one ask?"

"Mine." Buckingham twirled around as if he were a whirling dervish. "I found three traitors in the prince's train so I had them arrested. Lucky for you I happened to be in the vicinity." He leaned against the desk near to where I was lying and got a nail through his doublet. He jumped.

"And what now?" asked Richard. "First you dance around and then you jump about. Is this sports day?"

"Something scratched me," was Buckingham gloomy reply. Richard waved this complaint away:

"But let's get back to Pomfret castle, shall we, and to Earl Rivers, Lord Grey and Sir Vaughan. May I know what you propose to do with them now?" Buckingham looked flabbergasted.

"But we execute them, of course. You don't intend them to live in Pomfret forever, I hope. We may have other uses for the place."

"Execute them!" said Richard in a pensive voice, a finger at his lips. "And what, besides being people that you and I don't like, have they done? What are they accused of?" Buckingham picked an apple out of a fruit bowl and threw it into the air, catching it smartly.

"I'm sure we'll think of something," he said, as if he'd already lost interest in the whole matter.

"I see," said Richard again. "So. Chop off their heads. No due process. No trial. No possibility of defense. No evidence given, incriminating or otherwise." Buckingham looked at Richard in surprise.

"What are you on about? Due process? What the hell is that?"

"It is," came the reply, "making sure they are really guilty of committing the acts for which they are being executed." Buckingham shouted with laughter and had to sit down and wipe his face with his handkerchief.

"Oh, Richard, you'll be the death of me! This is not the way we do things in England. If you, as Lord Protector, say they are guilty, they are and off go their heads!" He leaned his hand on the desk then jumped away with a yelp. "Your cat bit me!" he shouted, enraged. "Guards, have this animal skewered and throw it into the latrine." But Richard held up his hands.

"Guards," he commanded sternly, "in the office of the Lord Protector, you obey only the Lord Protector." He turned to me and waggled his finger. "Don't do that again, Gaius, you'll get blood poisoning." Buckingham was enraged.

"What about me? What if I get blood poisoning?" I looked at Richard and read his thoughts: we should be that lucky. "Since when," screamed the victim, having now applied his handkerchief to staunch the blood, "is a cat more important that a Duke?" Richard ignored him and called:

"You, guard, go this instant and bring me Sir James Tyrrell." The guard dashed off. Richard turned to Buckingham: "I suppose you did bring Sir James back with you or is he also at Pomfret?" Buckighnam looked gloomy:

"Of course not. He hasn't done anything."

"I see," answered Richard, "well, that's all right then." Richard sat down and continued on his paperwork. Buckingham for the moment was nonplussed. He sat down too and gave me a venomous look. I looked back at him through slit eyes; he looked away first.

A clattering of feet brought Sir James Tyrrell into the room.

"Your Grace sent for me?" Richard laid his pen down.

"I did, Sir James. I want you to take twenty men, ride back to Pomfret castle and release Earl Rivers, Lord Grey and Sir Vaughn." Sir James' eyebrows shot up. Richard looked at him sharply. "Is there a problem?" he asked from behind lowered brows. Sir James shook his head.

"None at all, your Grace. What shall I tell the gentlemen?" Richard looked at me with arched eyebrows. I whispered:

"Nothing!"

"Nothing," said Richard firmly with an air of dismissal. Sir James just about ran out of the room. Richard shook himself like a large dog that had just dragged itself out of a stream. Then he got up, went over to Buckingham and put his arm around the other's shoulder.

"My dear Buckingham, let us not quarrel. Let us be cousins and allies. All I ask is that you do not take such serious steps without consulting me. There is a time for sowing and one for reaping. The death of those three would strengthen the Wydvilles and weaken our side." Buckingham looked at him doubtfully. Richard continued:

"I admit your cutting of corners, coz, has resulted in the prince now being in our sole custody. I would have preferred this to have happened in, shall we say, a smoother manner, if you get my meaning. You have given the Wydvilles reasons to break off from us for good and all. In the long run, a break was inevitable but I would have liked our truce to have held a bit longer. But what is done is done and cannot be undone and we shall have to make the best of it."

Buckingham squirmed but but then nodded:

"You are right, Richard. I acted in haste. Be assured I shall not do so again." Sounded nice, but I would keep an eye on Master Buckingham if I were Richard. Richard, however, seemed satisfied.

"And now, coz, we had better go and see the Prince and take things from there. Come along. You too, Gaius."

We piled into Richard's state coach. Buckingham sat as far from me as he could get.

"And where to, my dear Buckingham?" enquired Richard sweetly.

"The Guildhall," answered Buckingham expressionlessly. And off we set.

5.2 Into the Tower

The guildhall was packed: the Mayor of London and most of the aldermen, nobles such as Stanley, Hastings, Norfolk and Northumberland, churchmen by the dozen led by Cardinal Bouchier, heads of numerous guilds, important and not so important merchants and anyone else with the slightest right to be there and could be squeezed in.

The noise from so many voices was deafening. However, as Richard passed into the hall, a silence fell over the company and people stood aside, making a corridor to the back of the hall where the kid Edward sat on an improvised throne, looking unhappy and uncertain. Richard fell on one knee in front of the boy, getting up almost immediately. He opened his arms wide and Edward had to get up for the hug and a kiss on each cheek from his uncle.

"Your Grace, my dear very dear nephew, welcome to London." He held Edward at arm's length and looked him over. "My, how you've grown. Why, you're almost as tall as I am. But then, your parents are both tall." The kid Edward looked unfortable.

"Thank you, my uncle, and thank you for your care of me. Where is my family? And why did my uncle and brother stay at Pomfret Castle?" Richard was all smiles.

"I'm sure I can't say, your Grace, but they are following close behind you and will be here in a day or two. Your mother, now, and your brother and sisters will meet you later as they wanted to see you more privately, you could say, and not in the middle of this throng." His Grace looked crestfallen. I felt sorry for him. After all, he was just a kid. The Scots had it right – although long ago – the throne should pass to the strongest and most able warrior of the clan. Richard twirled about and said:

"Your Grace must be tired after so long a journey, so I propose you get some rest. I again apologize for not meeting Your Grace myself but I am sure the Mayor of London and the Cardinal have taken good care of you."

"It was indeed a wearisome road," replied the kid, managing to get away from Richard and sitting down, "and many unpleasant things happened along the way." Richard didn't say anything. I suppose he thought he had covered the subject earlier.

"But is my family all right?" asked Edward anxiously. Richard gave that loud laugh of his.

"All right? But of course they are all right. You'll see them soon enough. And, don't forget, I am your family also." And with that Edward had to be satisfied though his face looked glum. Richard clapped his hands and continued:

"But your travels are now quite in the past, dear nephew. Your Grace is in London, your capital city, safe and sound. Let us now proceed to the Tower where your Grace will be right royally installed." Richard turned to the company. "His Grace's entourage will follow us."

"Uncle, why am I going to the Tower?" Edward sounded more and more anxious. Richard laughed. His laugh was starting to get even on my nerves.

"Why, you will be staying in the royal chambers at the Tower of London, as tradition demands a king should before his coronation." Edward did not look molified. Richard clapped him on the shoulder, passed with him through the crowd, out of the guildhall, down the front steps and into the waiting state coach. I jumped in but Richard made sure Buckingham did not.

Upon reaching the Thames embankment, we left the coach and boarded a wonderful riverbarge, all floating pennents and oarsmen in royal livery, with Edward sitting on a throne on a raised dias, Richard standing behind him. Common folk crowded the banks, waving and calling out greetings as we sailed past and the kid waved back. In this way, we floated up the Thames in style. Even after having been up and down that river more times than I can count, I haven't become much of a sailor; in fact, I wouldn't go near the water if I could possibly avoid it. But it was a beautiful day and the river was smooth as a millpond.

The royal barge tied up at the imposing entrance to the fortress and everyone got it, following strict protocol, with Richard and the kid Edward in the lead. As there is no protocol for cats in royal processions, I walked right behind Richard. Edward was greeted by Sir Robert Brakenbury, Lieutenant of the Tower, of whom I had already heard much. He seemed a courtly old gentleman and I reluctantly had to agree that he looked honorable. At least, at first sight.

"Welcome, your Grace!" Sir Robert dropped on a creaky knee. He held out a large key. "And here is the key to the Tower, which is yours by right." The old man got up as Edward looked at Richard who guffawed.

"Just symbolic, my dear nephew." He smirked. "Even when you are a grown man, you will not want to have this dangling from your keyring."

After that bit of comedy, we passed into the Tower proper and climbed to the turret of the White Tower and the royal chambers. The rooms were imposing, all gilded furniture and chests with weird carvings, the bed covered with cloth of gold. Edward looked around but all that splendour did not seem to make him happy.

"And still no uncles," he said in a disappointed voice. "And no brother or mother." All this harping on uncles was making Richard irritated, I saw. But he kept his cool. The kid continued:

"Uncle," he whispered. "I do not like the Tower." Richard kneaded his hands.

"To be sure it's huge and, shall we say, gloomy with a bit damp here and there. Being so close to the river, you know. But it's strong, nephew. Remember: whoever holds the Tower holds all of London and England." I would have given Richard a failing grade for diplomacy and the kid was right on it.

"And who holds it now?" he asked.

"Why, I do, little nephew, in your name, as Lord Protector appointed by your father." This did not seem to comfort Edward to any great extent.

"They say Julius Caesar built the Tower," he inquired. "Is that true?" Richard scratched his head.

"If the learned professors say so, I fear we must believe them. I know that our joint ancestor, William the Conqueror, built what we see now. An impregnable fortress. Something to be proud of." Edward continued looking around. Beautiful tapestries, with scenes from the Old Testament, hung on each wall, in theory to keep out the cold seeping from the rock walls. One of them represented Abraham about to stab Isaac, the angel Gabriel hovering just above the sacrificial altar. I dug my claws into Richard's leg. He cried out, to the astonishment of all, and looked down.

"You moron," I whispered, "is that the kind of image you find suitable for the kid's chamber? He'll have frightful nightmares. Get rid of it." Richard looked at Isaac and called out immediately:

"Sir Brackenbury, surely we must have a more cheerful tapestry for the his Grace's chamber than this one. Take it away and find something a bit more suitable." A menial scuttled off at the behest of Sir Robert and in no time returned with one with the animals going two by two into Noah's ark. Richard beamed.

"Well, that's a lot better. But you are right, dear nephew. It will be lonely for you here, despite your army of retainers. I will see if I can persuade your mother, the dowager Queen, to allow your brother George to join you and keep you company. For the moment, I will leave your Grace to settle in. There is food and wine aplenty and a comfortable bed and so on. Tomorrow we shall speak further." Scraping and bowing, Richard left the chamber, the nobles following him. Sir Brakenbury and his staff took themselves off to their usual duties.

5.3 Another Meeting

A few days passed uneventfully. One morning Richard summoned me by pulling me out of a wardrobe where I had hidden myself against just such a move. That dratted Edward had ratted me out, of course. This kid, thinks I, will come to a bad end.

"No good hiding, Gaius. We have a meeting and you'd better be there." I trekked after him most unwillingly. On the other hand, I'd hate to be left out. He continued: "I didn't call it! Someone is taking a lot upon himself!"

We entered a large hall in the palace – medieval palaces seemed to be mostly large halls – with the usual scarred oak table. Richard took the seat at its head. An aide-de-camp had trickled in behind us.

"Mortimer," ordered Richard, "get us some drinks and snaquettes, would you. And, oh, send a messenger to Cardinal Boucher. Ask him, politely, mind you, to join us here. Have him wait in an ante-chamber and I will send for him." This taken care of, the others arrived: Lord Derby, the Duke of Buckingham, Lord Hastings and Sir Ratcliffe. Richard addressed Lord Derby:

"My Lord," he said, "you have called this meeting. Please let us know why." Lord Derby rose to his feet.

"My Lords, there has been a serious turn of events."

Buckingham interrupted him, giving me a malevolent look:

"Do we have to have the cat here?" Richard lifted his eyebrows:

"Bother you?" Buckingham shrugged but said nothing. Richard turned to Lord Derby.

"Lord Derby, please go on." Lord Derby sniffled, blew his nose on an ornate handkerchief, and did go on:

"Your Grace, the dowager Queen has sought sanctuary at Westminster Abbey, she and her children. And she has taken the Great Seal with her and as much treasure as she could carry." Richard frowned.

"What an extraordinary thing to do. Why on earth does she think she needs sanctuary? She and her family are not in danger." Lord Hastings cleared his throat.

"She now knows that her brother, son and Sir Vaughn were imprisoned in Pomfret Castle and it seems she fears for her and her children's safety." Richard got up, leaning his knuckes on the table top.

"What nonsense." Then he glared at Buckingham. "This is your doing, you fathead." He turned to the assembly. "And anyhow, that lot has been released."

"Oh," said Lord Derby in slight disappointment – he seemed to think the only good Wydville was a dead Wydville. "I didn't know that. Do you think they will come to London? If they do, then all the dowager Queen's fears would be put to rest." Richard shrugged:

"Personally, I don't think we'll see them around here anytime soon," he said. "Our pal Buckingham's little joke will have seen to that. But it would be best if the kid Richard joined his brother at the Tower, the boys should be together. It's not right that Edward should stay there all alone for God knows how long." Hastings stirred in his seat.

"I don't know why he's there to begin with." He looked around. Southhampton waved this away:

"All monarchs spend the night before their corronation in the Tower. That, if you like, is tradition." Hastings looked glum but said no more. Richard called to his equerry:

"Mortimer, could you see if Cardinal Bouchier has arrived? If so, please invite him to join us."

Cardinal Bouchier appeared immediately. After the usual bits of courtesy, Richard got down to brass tags:

"Your Eminence, I understand the dowager Queen has taken sanctuary at Westminster Abbey." The Cardinal nodded somberly; he was not a happy camper.

"That is so, my Lord; in fact, I have had to vacate my chambers for the dowager Queen and her daughters." Richard shook his head:

"I'm sorry to hear you've been turned out of your home like that. You must be well aware that there is no reason for the dowager Queen to seek sanctuary. As far as I, as Lord Protector, am concerned she is free to come and go as she likes." In the silence that follwed, I could feel that everyone was relieved the black spot had not descended on them. Richard continued:

"Would you be so kind, as my emissary, to carry the following message to the dowager Queen? That she has nothing to fear from me or from the Council and may take up her normal life wherever she wishes. There's no need for her to seek sanctuary at Westminster Abbey or anywhere else." Cardinal Bouchier said mildly:

"Perhaps if I could give her Grace a firm date for the coronation of the prince? That would do much to set her mind at ease." A bit of a silence. No one seemed keen to commit himself on this point. Finally, Hastings sang along:

"I agree with the Lord Cardinal. High time something was done." Richard ignored him and turned to the Cardinal:

"You may tell her Grace the Council will take her request under advisement and a date will be set; she will be the first to know." Cardinal Bouchier rose, bowed and turned to leave when Richard called him back:

"By the way, my lord Cardinal, while you are at it, please see that the Great Seal of England is returned to the Council. We cannot govern the realm without it or even plan the coronation. We will talk about the treasure she has unlawfully taken at another time." The cardinal took a further step towards the door but Richard wasn't done with him:

"Just a point more, my Lord Cardinal; tell her Grace that prince Edward is not happy in the Tower and feels lonely. It would be a kindness – and a step in the right direction – if she were to allow her other son Richard to join his brother." It was not a happy Cardinal who bowed himself out of the room, although he was happy enough to get away from this particular gathering.

Richard sat down, looked around and asked:

"Can we now discuss the coronation and perhaps set a date? The preparations will take long enough, as you all know, so the sooner we get on with it the better." Dead silence. "Well? And what now?"

Buckingham cleared his throat.

"Well, my dear Lord Protector," he said, steepling his fingers, "there is one more subject we need to discuss." Richard sighed and sat down.

"I suppose I'll have to listen," he said sourly, "or I'll be unable to sleep wondering what you're up to." One must say for Buckingham he had the hide of an ox. No way you could put him down and expect him to stay down.

"The question is," he said, "what kind of a country will we have when Edward is Edward V?" No one answered; everyone looked at Richard who said in surprise:

"What do you mean? What kind of country? Why, the one we've always had, with the peasants slaving away, the nobility stealing anything they can lay their hands on and the merchant classes getting richer and richer." Buckingham held up a finger.

"You are so right, my dear Lord Protector, I couldn't have put it better myself. But for one itsy bitsy point. By 'the nobility' you no longer mean the likes of us but also these parvenues, these nobodies, the Wydvilles and their faction." Richard threw up his arms.

"Don't, don't start on that again!"

"How long do you think you will be Lord Protector after Edward is crowned?" Buckingham leaned back in his chair and polished his nails on his doublet.

"I am Lord Protector by my brother's will and by the Council's consent until Edward is 18 years old." Buckingham tittered and Norfolk and Southhampton followed suit.

"That's what I love about Richard," interposed the Duke of Norfolk. "He thinks the best of everyone. However, Edward IV of blessed memory did not leave his will carved in stone."

"Yes, Norfolk," glowered Richard, "we all know about your little disagreements with my brother Edward. And about your hereditary title that he fleeced from you; I've told you it will be sorted."

"Will it now," Buckingham smiled sweetly, "once the council is filled with Wydvilles and their riffraff and you, although the first among equals, are only one voice among many." Richard turned on Buckingham.

"Are you implying," he snarled, "that the Wydvilles would dare to have me removed?"

"Once Edward is crowned," said the Duke of Southhampton, "consider it done." Richard looked at the aghast. He looked at me. I licked a paw.

"Makes sense," I murmured. "If you hold power for six years until Edward is 18, the Wydvilles will be history. Can't wait that long."

"So what do we do? Or rather, what would you people suggest?" It was the Duke of Norfolk who answered – I bet this was pre-arranged between him and Buckingham to make Buckingham's obnoxiousness less visible.

"Well, it's common knowledge, and your mother can attest to it, that your brother Edward had a pre-contract to marry what's her name, Lady Eleanor, daughter of the Earl of Shrewsbury." Richard seemed about to twist himself into knots.

"All that was ages ago, give me a break. If we bring this up now, everyone will say: why didn't anyone say something at the time? After all, Elizabeth has had an enormous number of children and the matter has never been an issue. And Eleanor married someone else anyway." He slammed his hand onto the table top; "If what you say is accepted as fact, my nephews would be bastards. No one would buy it!" I stretched myself and dug my claws into the oak surface. Buckingham moved back.

"Humans," I said slowly, "believe what is convenient to themselves. If the Wydvilles are unpopular enough and if people don't want them to rule England, why, they'll buy bastardy or anything else you come up with no matter how unlikely. After all, truth lies in the interests of the beholder." They all stared at me. "You realise, Richard," I continued, "that you need to fill all the main posts at once with people loyal to you – and to the Council, of course. Also, there is the little boy in the Tower. Just an afterthought." They all glared at me. So I continued: "On the other hand, possession, as has been so wisely stated, is nine-tenths of the law." Richard scratched his face as he often did when perplexed. But it was Lord Hastings who rose to his feet.

"I don't like this," he said. "There seems to be a conspiracy to usurp the crown from the legitimate heir."

"*'Woe to the kingdom,*" quoth I, "*that is ruled by a child'.*" They all stared at me. I elucidated: "*Ecclesiastics 10:16.* You can look it up if you don't believe me." Hastings snapped:

"And now we have to listen to Richard's cat laying out strategy and quoting the Bible! I'm sorry, but I stand for legitimacy! Nothing good ever came from shenanigans with the succession. We should have learned that over the past century. I say we keep to the letter of law and let the chips fall where they may." Richard said:

"In principle, I agree with Lord Hastings; however, before we go down that road, we all need to be on the same page – nobility and Wydvilles. The dowager Queen has plainly shown that she doesn't trust me – how much she hates me is common knowledge." I snickered;

"You can hardly have one without the other!" Richard glared and suddenly I felt slightly vulnerable. After all, as we'd already discussed, it's not too hard to kill a cat. But Richard's attention went back to the subject at issue:

"Let the dowager Queen leave sanctuary at the Abbey and return to her position at court and I, for one, will support Edward as king – as long as I am confirmed Lord Protector throughout his minority."

All this sounded wise and there were murmurs of agreement around the table. But Hastings got up and made for the door; Buckingham, rose and caught him by the arm.

"Your continued good health," he said softly, "depends on your being privy to every word said here." Hastings almost ran to his seat. Richard banged on the table with the flat of his hand.

"Now, Buckingham, that was totally uncalled for. We can't go around threatening people like that. Why, it'll give us a bad name." He looked flustered and perplexed. "And, anyway, I don't think the bastard idea is going to fly. If Edward is not to be king because he is a bastard, why, that rules out all his brothers and sisters. Then we come to Clarence's boy, Edward..."

"Another kid," said Norfolk, "but he is excluded by his father's attainder. Besides, he's a bit soft in the head."

"And that," I added, "leaves you, my dear Richard." Richard sat down, his mouth open.

"Don't be stupid. Who would ever agree to that?" Buckingham came back to the table.

"Each one of us," he said, "sitting round this table." And all but one member of those present rose and bowed in unison. "Hail, King Richard III."

"No, no, no," Richard swept his hand over the table top – if there had been anything on it would all have gone to the floor. "I don't want to be king. I want to go home to the North and live quietly with my wife and son."

"Noblesse oblige," intoned Norfolk.

"And *Honi soit*," I added, "*qui mal y pense*."

"Look," said Richard, "this is all very well. I don't like the Wydvilles any more than you do. But how many Wydvilles are there? 20? 30? And how many Englishmen are there?" No one knew since the last census had been taken by William the Conqueror. "If I am to become king, the people must ask me to take the crown. And it must be approved by Parliament. Otherwise, you can forget it and start looking for pleasant exile spots. Come along, Gaius, let's go."

But of course, this would all have been too easy. Trouble there must be and trouble came from our friend, Lord Hastings. He was all aflame and couldn't keep still. While he danced about, he shouted, pointing at Richard:

"Lord Protector, is it? So, with the help of that thing," and he pointed to Buckingham who was standing with his mouth wide open, "you plan to make yourself king!" A few more pirouettes. "Lord Protector is not enough for you! But you seem to forget yourself. The throne belongs to my friend Edward's sons, not to you … your misshapen fiend!"

This was rough stuff. I wondered how Hastings dared. After all, he knew all about the Tower, having been a guest there himself. Richard goggled at him.

"Misshapen, do you say?" he shouted back. "You must be out of your mind. So, I have one shoulder higher than the other – and what's that to do with the price of eggs? Misshapen? Why, I participated in all those foul battles which I could hardly have done had I been misshapen." Buckingham finally found his voice.

"William, William," he said, putting a meaty arm around Hastings, "you mustn't carry on like this, you really mustn't. The Council had agreed that Edward's marriage to Elisabeth is invalid, due to Edward's earlier pledge to Lady Thingummy!" The furious Hastings now turned on poor Buckingham.

"You, you always were a scoundrel and now you are also a traitor! This pledge is all poppycock and well you know it!" He spun around and pointed at Richard? "And you know it!" But Buckingham had now found his stride.

"Richard, could you have someone bring in a snortful for poor William? I really think he needs something to steady his nerves. The time he spent in the Tower has unhinged him. Poor fellow, to fall prey to Ma Wydville! And to be betrayed by his best friend, Edward, who, without a thought of their long friendship, signed the warrant as his concubine asked him to do." This was a nasty one, although it was all some time ago. However… The needful having arrived, everyone had a drink. Even I needed something.

This type of quarrel among humans is always unsettling for a cat. How many psychopaths have started out on their killing sprees by going first for a neighbor's cat? I jumped hastily off the table and hid under a massive oak chest.

Now, Richard is usually a good tempered fellow but even he thought that Hastings was beyond the pale. Having had his own snortful, he turned to Hastings.

"You forget, my friend, your pledge to me as Lord Protector. You even seem to have forgotten that you supported me against those vile Wydvilles. What's all this about now?" Hastings went berserk.

"It's the law, you blasted creature! It's the law I want upheld!" Richard shook his head.

"Nonsense, it's not the law, it's the custom!" He faced Hastings. "And where was the law, as you call it, when you agreed to the execution of Henry VI, who was, without a doubt, anointed and crowned king of England? Where were your priorities then? Or is the law only important when you say so?" Hastings got even more furious.

"Henry VI was a usurper! Edward, my friend Edward was the real King!" Richard sighed:

"Perhaps, if we go all the way back to Edward III!"

"You yourself fought against him!" cried Hastings. But Richard was adamant.

"I fought for my family, not against Henry VI!" Well, I thought. I suppose it's possible. Now Northumberland joined in the fray.

"Richard," he called out, "why don't we put Hastings in the Tower until he cools down!"

"Yes," agreed Southampton, "we can't do with all this shouting and carrying on. And Hastings already knows the way."

Richard told me later he had really seen no alternative. Hastings had inherited Edward IV's mistress, Jane Shore, who was very handsome but also very unscrupulous. And dappled in witchcraft now and again. Richard thought that Jane may have put Hastings up to it in defense of her dead lover.

As I curled up to sleep, I reviewed all that had happened at the meeting. For all Richard's bluster about legitimacy and succession, he was clearly sitting on the fence. Most of the others, *pace* Lord Hastings, seemed to have already made up their minds: a kid on the throne – any kid – is a damned liability, an unknown quantity, a malleable tool in the hands of cunning grown-ups; a disaster waiting to happen.

5.4 Maximum Security

That next evening, Richard and I sat down for a little chat.

"Richard," I said, "listen, please, because this is very serious. You have one kid in the Tower and and Ma Wydville has lost her wits and is sending you her spare, Richard, and in consequence you will now have two. We know it's on the cards that there isn't going be a coronation anytime soon, at least for Edward." Richard shook his head impatiently but I held up a paw. "Don't argue. I'm telling you those two boys will be in very grave danger indeed."

"What kind of danger?" cried Richard, "they'll be locked up in the Tower! I have guards all over the place who are all loyal to me." I sneered:

"Don't make me laugh, Richard. Loyal to you, forsooth. Count on people's unswearing loyalty and see where it'll get you. Also, the question isn't the number or type of guards, whether armed with axes, lances, swords or whatnot." Richard now got really impatient.

"Well, Gaius, have your say and be quick about it. I'm worn out." It was now Happy Hour and I suggested Richard get some wine for himself and water for me. After that had been arranged, the minion left, leaving the bottle, shutting the door after him at my insistence. Having lapped my water, I said:

"You will agree, Richard, that there are factions who would like to remove these kids from the Tower or even from the planet Earth. You could say that those two kids are the rarest, hence the most valuable, commodity in England at the moment. Have you any idea of what they would be worth in gold on the open market?" Richard refilled his goblet.

"Gaius, you're losing you mind! Why do I listen to you? You're just a cat. And what's a commodity?" I thought a bit. I'd made a faux past. Commodity was as real to Richard as rocket science. I sighed and gave it a try.

"It is," I explained, "a physical substance, in our case the princes, which is interchangeable with another product of the same type [say, another claimant to the English throne] or for hard cash; investors buy or sell commodities usually through futures contracts. That is, you give me cash today for something I don't have, but that I expect to get soon, at which time I will give it to you." I scratched my chin in thought, then continued:

"The price of a commodity is subject to the laws of supply and demand; but in the matter of Yorkist princes we, so to speak, have the market cornered and the sky is the limit as far as price goes – the buyer will pay anything for something he can't be sure of getting, so his risk is immense Still, I don't think we'd lack willing buyers, no matter our terms, if we brought our goods to market."

"Gaius," snarled Richard, "I am starting to lose my mind. Why do I listen to you?"

"You will listen because my species has never lost its sense of danger. And the danger here, my friend, is huge. Humans think they're safe because they happen to be a prince or a duke or live in a castle with high walls or have a dog. Cats have learned over six million years to be wary, to be carefully, to choose the wisest course in any given situation – fight or flight – an instinct you humans have lost." Richard threw wide his arms.

"You are making less and less sense. Six million years! Everyone knows the world has existed for about four thousand years. Look at the Bible. Do the sums."

"The human species can be four thousand years old, if you like," I answered witheringly, "but we felines go back at least six million. The Bible is nothing to us except a fat book of doubtful authenticity." He gave it up. To tell the truth, I think the millions floored him. I pressed my advantage.

"Richard, no one is safe, especially two snotty kids, when a whole kingdom is at stake. It's a bit like the Tower. Whoever is in possession has the advantage. " Richard got to his feet impatiently.

"But they are in the Tower, or will be tomorrow, which, as we know, is impregnable, so I hold the advantage." I scratched the cushion I was lying on; silver threads came out.

"To the army outside, Richard, to the army outside. Not to the traitor within."

"Traitor?" shouted Richard. "Sir Brakenbury? Don't make me laugh." I waggled a paw at him.

"This is no laughing matter, pal. Forget for the moment Sir Brakenbury. And think of the valets, chefs, kitchen maids, scullions, boot boys, serving boys, maids, upstairs, 'tween and downstairs, that form a prince's household, to say nothing of guards, and each single one of them, Richard, each has his or her price. Each can be bought for a shilling or two.

"To do what, you may ask. Take a message, copy a key in wax, open a door, or throw down a rope, you name it. Each person in that Tower with access to the princes is a threat to their lives and to your Protectorship or Kingship, should you decide to go for that." Richard looked cowed. Then he sighed and sat down and rubbed his face. I could see he was giving up.

"So, tell me what you would have me do." I jumped down and had a roll on the floor. No carpets, thank God. I have a horror of lice.

"As soon as the kid Richard arrives at the Tower, which should be tomorrow, you must get rid of their retinue, the whole lot." Richard was horrified.

"But princes can't live without servants!" I snorted.

"Of course they can. But they won't have to, not altogether. Laundry, for instance; not that I expect they will want their clothes washed all that often, from what I can see of present hygienic standards. But laundry can be done by Tower servants, wife of a jailer, say. Sir Robert should go through every piece and make a complete list when it's taken and thoroughly checked when it's returned. Likewise, food should be prepared in the Tower's common kitchen..."

"The princes can't eat the same food as the common soldiers!" objected Richard aghast. I ignored the interruption.

"... and all meals should be taken by the princes with Sir Robert and the tutor, who should either be totally faithful to you or scared stiff of you. Food should be served in common pots that the four will share." Richard threw up his hands.

"Gaius, royalty can't live like that." I waved his comment away.

"As for cleaning: dusting, sweeping out rushes and turning down beds, the boys can be taken into the garden while this is being done, again by females from the Tower staff. They must be searched by Sir Robert before and after ..."

"Sir Robert is not going to like this!"

"...and Sir Robert should search the room thoroughly after the kids leave it and before they are let in again." Richard covered his face with his hands, shaking his head. I went on: "And no one, but no one, should have access to the boys but you, Sir Robert and their tutor, who should never ever be allowed to leave the Tower. Any correspondence he sends or receives should go to you first so you can see what he's up to. Don't trust that guy an inch."

"Perhaps," snarled Richard, "you'd like to check the Tower correspondence yourself."

"No," I said calmly, lying down. "I can't read. The unfortunate fact is that we must be able to trust someone and that someone must be Sir Robert, whom you claim to be an honorable man. Have you got the guts to bet your life on it?"

"Gaius, this is absurd!"

"Never mind that. Do you trust Sir Robert as an honorable man?" Richard stalked about the room, waiving his hands.

"I do! And you say I must." I nodded sagely.

"Ahh… but that's for you to find out and I hope you won't." I bit on one of my nails for a moment and then went on.

"Also, I've observed there is only one door leading to the White Tower where the boys are kept. Be sure there is only one key, to be held by Sir Robert, whom, at your valuation, I take to be an honest man. You can have as many guards as you like by the door, but only Sir Robert enters."

"Gaius, this is inhuman," cried Richard. I looked surprised.

"Naturally. I am a cat. I think in non-human terms, lucky for you. I trust no one, I like no one. It's called instinct or, if you like, the survival of the best prepared. But take it whichever way suits you. If those kids are poisoned, disappear, if the Wydvilles or another faction gets hold of them, you, my friend, will be history."

Richard sighed and walked out. There were many other things I could suggest: surveillance cameras, for one, wire taps, snipers, infrared lights and SWAT teams, FBI agents in wrapout sunglasses, but that would be just a waste of time. So I lay down, stretched out and had a well deserved nap.

5.5 A Weekend at the Tower

Much to everyone's surprise, Cardinal Bouchier duly went to Westminster and asked Ma Wydville if the kid Richard could join Edward in the Tower. Personally, had I been Elisabeth, I would have hung on to that second kid tooth and nail. She did her best – cried and carried on, about how much Gloucester hated her and how he planned to destroy her and her whole family and how it was all a plot to make himself, Gloucester, king.

But she finally gave way, one can only wonder why, and the Cardinal brought the kid Richard to Westminster. I may add, together with the Great Seal. Of course, Richard the elder was all over the kid in proper uncle fashion, showering him with kindness and sweets and whatever else one uses to buy the goodwill of children, which is, alas, all too easy.

I went with Richard when he took the kid Richard to the Tower. I sat in a window embrasure during the somewhat embarrassing scene that followed. Richard the elder tried to be a very genial, very loving uncle. But the kids were both skeptical and frightened, as well they might have been.

"Well, lads," said the uncle with a big smile, "so here we are. Our two boys together. Won't that be jolly?"

"How long are we going to stay here?" asked Richard. "Why can't we both stay with mother at Westminster?" Richard looked embarrassed but soon bounced back:

"You see, boys, your mother is staying in the Archbishop's palace. With all your sisters. I can never keep track of them. It would be difficult to squeeze you both in, too, and it would be an imposition on the poor Archbishop, who has already been turned out of house and home." Gay laughter from Richard the elder. Seeing the stony faces before him, he continued:

"There's no reason for everybody to be so crowded. There's plenty of space here. Don't you think this is a lovely chamber? An enormous bed, canopy, curtains and all. Chests for all your things. Tapestries on all the walls. Fresh rushes on the floor every day, I do assure you. Windows looking out over wonderful vistas." Entirely the wrong thing to say to kids. "And there is a fully equipped and well lighted schoolroom next door." No cheers for the schoolroom. Richard the elder turned to Edward.

"Well, my dear nephew," I noticed that Richard never used Edward's putative title. "Aren't you happy to have your brother here? You have been complaining about being alone so much." Edward squirmed.

"Of course it's nice to have Richard with me," he answered carefully. "But I miss my mother and my other uncles." Richard the elder gave another great false laugh.

"Uncles! Why, my dear nephew, one can have too many uncles, just ask Henry VI." I cleared my throat and Richard the elder saw he'd stepped in it. More smiles: "Too many uncles definitely spoil the broth, boys. Some uncles, yes, many uncles, umm, not so good."

"But mother, when can I see mother?"

"Soon, very soon, my dear nephew, just as soon as it can be arranged." This sounded ominous to me but I'm not a stupid kid but a smart cat. Edward sat down on the bed and sighed.

"Uncle, aren't I going to be king?" More forced laugher from the elder Richard.

"Oh, dear, oh, dear, my boy. Being king is a man's game and a dangerous game at that. Leave that to your elders for the time being and who knows what will happen in the future?"

"But I should be king," insisted the moronic kid. "I am my father's eldest son and I should follow my father on the throne as ordained by God." Richard put his arm around his sulking nephew.

"Do you know, my boy, that in the Bible is says: *Woe to the land whose king is a child.* That you are your father's son is indisputable; if you are the heir to the throne, well, there might be a slight difficulty there."

Edward jumped up. Snotty little idiot. I suppose it's the public school education that makes the upper classes so arrogant and stupid.

"What do you mean by that, uncle?" But Richard the elder had had enough. He got up, placing a hand on the shoulder of each child.

"One day we will speak of this, my boys, but not today, not today. Be sure that here you are safe and nothing evil can touch you. You have the best quarters of any noble in the land – this is the coronation suite, you know, and there is the beautiful garden where you can play every day if you like." Yeah, as long as it wasn't raining, which was about once a month. Richard the kid rushed forward and grabbed Richard the elder's hand:

"Uncle, can your cat stay with us for a while? We'd look after him really well and play with him all the time." I covered my eyes with my paws. Oh, Lord of cats, I don't deserve this. Richard looked at me uncertainly.

"Well," he said slowly, "he's not, so to speak, my cat. Cats, you know, don't belong to anyone but themselves and they never do anything they don't want to do. Let's ask him."

"Ask a cat!" sneered Edward. "Really, uncle! You're the Lord Protector and everyone must do as you say." Richard the elder waggled his finger.

"That is very true," he said, "if you are talking about people. But cats are different. So I will ask him."

He turned to me. I uncovered my eyes and our eyes met. There was pleading look in Richard's.

"Gaius," he said, "I'm sure you'll be happy to stay here for a few days and play with the boys." I was about it issue a *nolle proseque*[4] but then looked at the kid Richard's expectant face.

"I suppose so," I answered none too politely. "If you put it that way." Both kids stared.

"He speaks," cried Edward. "Can you speak, Gaius?" I crossed my paws and yawned.

"Of course I can speak," without any further explanation. Richard the elder clapped his hands.

"Jolly good, jolly jolly good. I'll come and pick you up in a few days, Gaius." With more pats and smiles he got himself out of the door as fast as he could. I sighed. But I suppose I can take a few roughs with a smooth or two.

---

4   Not on your life

If I had known what was in store for me, I would have run all the way back to my beach in Niteroi in the 21st century. But, although I could see the far away future, I could not look into the next few days.

Of course, the boys wanted to carry me around and pet me all day long. But I soon put a stop to that with a hiss or two and a well-placed scratch here and there and after that we got on famously. But it was hard work, let me tell you. Unfortunately for me, all that weekend the sun shone from an unblemished sky. Every morning I looked for clouds, heavy with rain and every morning I was disappointed. So into the garden we went to 'play'.

We played tag. Sometimes I chased them, sometimes they chased me. A human can't catch a cat that doesn't want to be caught but sometimes I let them win just to keep things exciting. We played hide and seek but I put down my paw on the version *count to one hundred* and shout *coming, ready or not*. It's not that I'm a spoilsport but I can only count to ten, the number of my front claws. I usually won because a cat can get in almost anywhere but a few times I heard shrill laughter:

"Edward, I've found him, his tail is sticking out!" Rats! That's one drawback to being a cat, one's not always certain where one's tail is.

The kids threw sticks for me to chase, as if I were a dog, Lord of cats support me. But chase sticks I did. And leaves drifting in the wind and butterflies who complained bitterly saying I was upsetting their mealtimes. There were birds also, of course, that I was supposed to hunt and catch. I soon came to an agreement with the locals; I would chase them; they fluttered and chirped and pretended to be scared to death, the boys whooping and cheering me on; I even caught some but somehow they always managed to get away.

But the kids' favourite game was making me climb a tree and then they would go shouting for their tutor, Master William Slaughter.

"Master Slaughter, Master Slaughter," they would cry, "Gaius is stuck in the tree and can't get down. Please come and help him." So there was a great commotion, the kids ran into a potting shed and got a rickety old ladder and poor Master Slaughter would climb up, very unwillingly and very unsteadily, until he had almost reached the branch I was clinging to. Then I would run down the tree and he would, swearing and shaking, begin laboriously to climb down and, to the great joy of the boys, usually falling off and hollering that his back was broken and he was going to complain to the Lord Protector of the behaviour of both princes and cat. Well, he could do that until the moon turned blue for all the good it would do him.

In the evenings, after supper, we played *hunt the slipper*, and I won every time. Nose for nose, humans don't even come close to a cat when it comes to sniffing things out.

As it was weekend and there were no lessons, I got no chance for a bit of shut-eye until bedtime when I would fall exhausted onto the bed with the boys to their great delight and the disgust of their tutor, Master Slaughter, who said severely:

"A cat in the princes' bed. So unhygienic." This, mind you, from someone who only changed his small clothes at Whitsun and as far as anyone knew had never taken a bath in his life. But I was too tired to care about him – as far as beds went, considering that this was the 16th century, it was the best that could be had. Mattress stuffed with straw and pillows with feathers. I tried not to think of bed bugs, lice and other unspeakables, to say nothing of things that went bump in the night. I was too tired to stay awake to entertain or chase anything and as far as I was concerned, they could get on with it, whatever 'they' were.

One night I felt a poke in my tummy – I was sleeping on my back, all four paws in the air, an amazingly comfortable position; I opened half an eye and saw it was Edward. Richard was asleep, all tucked up, clinging to some kind of toy.

"Gaius, Gaius," whispered Edward, "are you awake?"

"Well, I am now," I answered grumpily. "What is it? Got a tummy ache? Can't help you."

"Gaius," said Edward in a sort of dreamy voice, "would you like to be a king?" A stupid question if I ever heard one.

"I am a king," I answered turning to the other side and hoping the kid would shut up. Edward sniggered.

"You can't be king, Gaius, you're a cat." I sighed. Socratic disputations with a kid in the middle of the night at the Tower of London? I think not.

"Kid," I said, "anyone who owns the sky and the sea and the trees and the flowers and the mountains and the fields is a king." A slight silence.

"You own all that?" the voice was very doubting.

"I do," I answered firmly. "And so does every creature on the planet, except the king." Thoughtful pause.

"I don't think I understand."

"I mean," I said, "that any time I want to look at the sky, count the stars, run in the meadows, sniff the flowers or listen to the birds sing I can do so. No one says I'm not to look at the sky because it belongs to the king. That's what I mean by being a king. Freedom to enjoy the world or such bits as I want. No responsibility, no accountability." Another pause.

"But the king can do anything!" I sneered.

"Oh, puleese. A king can't do anything like that. If he wants to run in the meadows, he has to take a dozen courtiers plus a dozen soldiers with him in case he should meet a bad man. Is that freedom? He can cut off someone's head and so what? After he's done that, the victim is beyond his power. Victim wins. A king can live in a palace – with about 2,000 other people – the crowds would drive me insane. As for the sanitation ..." I shuddered.

"A king is hardly ever alone – there is always somebody there, supposedly to keep him safe but in truth taking away his freedom to come and go. And he has no friends. People who surround a king just want to take advantage of his position for their own gain. King? I'll take my kind of liberty any day of the week. More fool you if you want to be king."

"But it has been ordained by God that I should be king!"

"Now, don't be blaming the greed of humanity on some sort of divinity. If there is a God, he'd be very pissed off. Remember: *do not take the name of the Lord in vain.* Tell me, Edward, do you want to be a king? Listen to this:

> *... rounds the mortal temples of a king*
> *Keeps Death his court and there [death] sits,*
> *Scoffing [the kingly] state and grinning at [the kingly] pomp,*
> *Allowing [the king] a breath, a little scene,*

To monarchize, be fear'd and kill with looks,
Infusing [the king]with self and vain conceit,
As if this flesh which walls about our life,
Were brass impregnable, and humour'd thus.
[Death]comes at the last and with a little pin
Bores through his castle wall, and farewell king!"[5]

I stopped and looked at him – don't forget that cats can see in the dark. I'm not sure he took it all in but then he said:

"I thought a King was God's anointed."

"Ah," says I, "there's the rub, little friend, because Death – not God – plays the tune and all us living creatures dance to it. And, as far as Death is concerned, you're no better than the meanest scullion in the kitchen." Another pause. A long one this time. Then Edward said:

"I think you made that up!" I sneered again:

"Do you think that I, an ordinary moggie, could have come up with such a speech? But thanks for your confidence. These are the words of Richard II, King of England. You've heard of him, I take it?" Actually, Richard II was probably too stupid to have made this lyrical speech but Will Shakespeare says he did and that's good enough for me. Edward answered uncertainly.

"Yes... He became king when he was still a boy."

"And ended up as we all know. Boy kings seldom turn out well. No offence." Edward brooded as well he might. Then he said:

"But I shan't be like Richard II. If I live to be a man and a king, I'll win back our ancient rights in France or die a soldier as I lived a king." I wanted to bury my head under the pillow. Humans are so infernally stupid. Lord of cats, give me patience. I even missed Eddie. I said:

"Do you think you'll be able make strategic decisions or command soldiers in the field?"

"Well, not right away! But later on, when I'm old enough."

"I don't want to be a pessimist, Edward, but I think your chances of reaching the age you term as 'old enough' to be 50-50. Not good

---

[5]   *Richard II*: Wm Shakespeare

odds." There was a long silence and I was almost asleep when I thought of something else.

"As for, as you put it, *ancient manorial rights* in France. Are you willing to destroy your kingdom to follow such a chimerical dream? You know what happened to Henry V? Do you think he made a good choice by abandoning his kingdom to follow a dream in France?"

"But France is ours by right." What an idiot boy. I said.

"No, it isn't. France belongs to the French, to the people who live there. They don't care for ancient manorial rights, yours or anyone else's. And, anyway, your supply lines would be too long. Fighting a battle across the sea is lost before it begins. Ask the Americans about Vietnam."

"Who about what?"

"Well, never mind."

"But you forget the glory of Agincourt!" The kid's head was full of dreams of knights and battles and so on.

"Agincourt! Do you want to make me laugh? A battle was won because the French were greater idiots than the English. All hail the conquering hero. But at the end of the day, your lot lost the war. What then the price of battles won?" There was silence for a bit. Then Edward said:

"I don't think I like you very much."

"Fine," was my answer, "I don't care if you like me or not. That's how cats are: if you like them, they might, just might, like you back. But if you don't, the cat doesn't care." After a pause, a question in the dark:

"You don't think I should be king, do you?"

"I think you should be a kid and enjoy yourself and go to school and play games and leave the nasty bits to the grownups."

"Do you think uncle Richard would believe me if I said I didn't want to be king?"

"Uncle Richard is not a problem, kid, your mother is."

"My mother?"

"Yeah. Go to sleep. Que sera será."

True to his word, Richard came and picked me up three days later. The boys begged for me to stay but Richard was firm. He needed me back – for what, he didn't explain and the boys seemed to assume there was a plague of mice in his chamber or some such thing.

As our barge headed towards the palace, I said to Richard:

"You can't leave those kids in the Tower forever, Richard. Something has to be done." He raised his eyebrows:

"I'm open to suggestions, Gaius." I cleared my throat. I was going to suggest sending them to the American colonies but remembered in time that Cristopher Columbus hadn't been born yet. And the East India Company hadn't been incorporated. The Crusades were over and even Martin Luther wasn't around. Botany Bay? A long way in the future. So what did people do with undesirable young men in those days?

"You could sell them at the slave market in Constantinople," I said lamely, which got me a nasty look and the remark:

"Don't be ridiculous, Gaius!"

I confess I felt guilty about leaving those kids. I also missed them and felt sorry for their plight. So alone, so vulnerable to the storms the grownups were raising around them. Truly, childhood should be a sacred thing; it is so short and soon enough the real world closes in and the innocent joys of children – a garden with flowers, butterflies and birds and an unwilling cat for entertainment – remains only a dream if remembered at all.

6
Richard for king!

6.1 With a little bit of spin

Not too far away from Westminster, since London wasn't much of a city in those days, what could be called an informal Council meeting had been convened. Informal because Richard, the Lord Protector, hadn't been invited. The usual suspects were there, Buckingham, Derby, Norfolk, Northumberland, Surrey, as well as lesser figures such as Sir James Tyrrel, Sir William Catesby and Sir Richard Ratcliffe, these last three staunch Richard men. Buckingham took, so to speak, the chair.

"My friends," he said, "we have come to a crossroads in our affairs. It is vital that Richard of Gloucester be king of England if we are to have any peace and continue to prosper and enrich ourselves. Edward V means the Wydvilles and the Wydvilles mean disaster for us."

"Hear, hear," murmured Derby, who was sitting sideways in his chair, a most uncomfortable position. Buckingham ignored him.

"I have gone as far – and you will understand how desperate I think our case is – of having brought Richard's cat with me." Everyone looked at me as I lay on the table, assessing each one as possible future prey.

"Nonsense," blustered Norfolk, "what good will a cat do anyone?"

"Well, whether we like it or not," retorted Buckingham, "this cat has Richard's ear and seems to know Richard's mind. Because, and I cannot stress this too much, Richard is very reluctant to be king, although he has no more love for the Wydvilles than we do." I lifted my head and looked each man in the eye.

"A disputed throne," I said, "leads to civil strife and a king considered to be a usurper usually does not last long. You've seen that already. So why should Richard stick his neck out?" Buckingham looked nonplussed. But Norfolk pitched in:

"For the good of the realm," he said assertively. I lifted my head:

"Gentlemen, the good of the realm would be achieved if each little country town handled its own affairs. And, of course, abolishing religion to get rid of the grasping priests who never seem to have enough. But I take it this is not the way you want to go." No one bothered to answer. Buckingham, however, asked me:

"What, in your opinion, would it take to convince Richard to become king?" I sat up as the subject was getting more serious, curling my tail around my paws. I said:

"I take it you want Richard to be king because you feel you can manipulate him. If so, I would be careful. Richard is not as soft as he looks." Norfolk gave me a disgusted look.

"Nonsense," he said, "such a thing never occurred to us. We feel that, in the present crisis, he is by far the best candidate."

"By crisis, you mean your tug-of-war with the Wydvilles. With the kid Edward on the throne, you wouldn't stand a chance of getting back the estates Edward IV stole from you or in general bettering yourselves." I sniggered. "If I were to advise you guys, I would say: *boys, why don't you lie low until this whole thing has blown over.* If you kept to your various castles or whatever, I should imagine the Wydvilles could be neutralized. Because, and note this well, my friends, when it comes to call up an army, it is you, the landed nobility, who have the means: men. The crown, especially on the head of the kid Edward, is nowhere. The crown, you might say, has no real power base." They looked at each other.

"What do you mean by a 'power base'" asked Ratcliffe.

"It is," I said, "people who are loyal to you because they live in your villages or on your land or for any number of reasons such as family, tradition, and so on. The crown, especially now, has none of this. Any real loyalty to the crown was destroyed by the civil war and the unedifying sight of all those royal descendents killing their kith and kin. The whole kingdom, to my mind, is up for grabs." They exchanged looks. I would say that they hadn't had any training in political sciences. I lay down again, adding:

"The crown's stronghold is London. Whoever holds London holds the crown and whoever is king in London holds the realm."

"Exactly," said Suffolk. "And who holds London today?"

"Why, Richard," answered Buckingham impatiently.

"So," I drawled, "if any of you lot wanted to be king, you would have to wrest London from Richard. But one thing is certain: the Wydvilles cannot do that." Hastings frowned:

"And why not?"

"Because," I said, "London holds the Tower and the Tower holds the Wydvilles hopes for the crown. With the two kids in the Tower, the Wydvilles are neutralized." Norfolk banged the table with his fist. Given the hardness of the oak, he must have hurt his hand.

"Now this is where we started out. How do we convince Richard to take the crown?" Everyone looked at me.

"You need," I answered, "to make him believe it is the only possible solution."

"And how should that be done?"

"By popular acceptance or acclaim, if you wish." They gasped. I continued hurriedly. "I don't mean that every Englishman should vote for him; though ideal, this isn't part of your present reality. The foremost London commoners, Lord Mayor, guild leaders, merchants and that sort, should beg him to take the crown."

They chewed on that for a bit. I sighed. By themselves, they weren't going to get anywhere. Suffolk said slowly.

"The trouble is that some factions of the population feel that Edward is the legitimate heir and should be crowned."

"So, there you have it, the weak point," I said. "What you need is a bit of spin."

"Spin!" Buckingham frowned. "What's spin?"

"It's when you put a favourable slant to an item of news, potentially an unpopular policy, on behalf of a political personality. You try to forestall negative publicity by spreading a favourable interpretation of words or actions of a person in power. If you like, a distinctive point of view, emphasis or interpretation of a given fact." More blank looks. Oh, dear.

"Now, you'll remember that someone – can't remember who – tried to discredit Edward IV, implying he wasn't the son of the Duke of York but a blow-by from an affair of the Duchess, his mother, with an archer." Norfolk shook his head:

"Well, Richard shot that one down since it would implicate his mother." Heads nodded.

"Right," I remarked, "that didn't fly. But there's another one – that Edward IV was pre-contracted to some girl or other, thereby making his marriage to Elizabeth Wydville invalid and her kids all bastards." Buckingham tapped his fingers on the table.

"Yes," he said slowly, "if that were known far and wide, it would certainly tarnish the Wydville family and especially Elisabeth's children. It could bring up the spectre of another civil war. However, a strong, mature and seasoned king would make the realm feel safe. But how do you do it, this spin?"

"Easy," I said, "send all your servants and adherents and go yourselves and spread this story of Edward's pre-contract about, in alehouses, hostels, markets, fairs, in fact everywhere and anywhere; also, how, with a child on the throne, war would be more or less inevitable. And sing Richard's praises high and loud in all quarters as the man who will save the day." I stretched. "And, by the way, don't forget to get the approval of Parliament." The Duke of Norfolk's mouth gaped:

"You gotta be kidding." I shook my head.

"I am not. Take my word for it, without this, Richard won't buy in." And so the meeting was over; everyone got up and I could see their thoughts as if they'd written them down on a blackboard: *'why should we believe this stupid cat?'* But since no one tried answering this question and they were out of options, they went off, I suppose, to do their various things.

6.2 Enter Rumour

I was lying on Richard's work table while he was beavering away, harrowing his poor clerks to death, calling for documents while a secretary tried to set up an agenda for the next four weeks or so. It seems that brother Edward had spent his last year with a finger on the executioner's pulse ignoring whatever else needed to be done. Interesting that the Wydvilles took no interest at all in the day-to-day administration of the realm. That, believe you me, is the way to power - anywhere. If you're willing to do someone else's work for them, they will soon find themselves out of a job and you'll be lording it over them.

With the iron grip he now had on the running of the realm, it would be difficult to pries Richard lose from power; he seemed to have a real talent for management and made short work of the messes Edward had left behind. He was a bit of a ruthless taskmaster – anyone working for him worked as long as he did – which was well into the night. Needless to say, he was not popular with the palace staff. Richard's favorite question to underlings was: "You say it cannot be done? It can be done and it will be done so get on with it!" in a fierce and intense voice, sending the culprit scuttling off to do whatever it was he had just told Richard couldn't be done.

All this activity made me feel very tired; the air outside was cool and I soon decided that an open window would be a more pleasant spot for serious napping and moved to a convenient embrasure. But of course it couldn't last. At one point, Richard said:

"Gaius, come here and witness my signature on this warrant." I almost fell off the window ledge.

"Are you trying to be funny?" I was not amused.

"No," said Richard. "Just dip your paw into the ink. No one will ever notice." I bristled:

"I think not. My paw would get covered in ink which I am not about to lick off." Richard picked me up by the scruff of my neck – so undignified but it's one position from which a cat can't fight – and set me down next to his infernal document.

"Just dip your claws in the ink and scratch next to my name, here." Well, I could do that. I could alway wipe my claws on one of the priceless tapestries. Richard and I looked at the result. "Perfect," he said, and put it away. Would you guess that historians in the 20th century are still trying to discover which noble witneseed that particular signature? The guy has a lifetime job.

It was now happy hour. Richard had his staff well trained and on the dot a menial came running in with wine for Richard and water for me. He picked up his tumbler, came over to my window and sat down in a wooden armchair, filled with beautifully embroidered cushions. Whether by Anne, his wife, or Ma Wydville I couldn't say.

"I don't like it," he said, shaking his head sadly, "not one bit. It doesn't seem right." I opened one eye and asked:

"What on earth are you talking about?"

"All this talk of Edward and Elisabeth not being properly married and all those kids being illegitimate."

"But you know all about that," I said, "it was discussed, if I remember rightly, at a number of Council meeting; you weren't at the last one but I told you what happened."

"Yes, yes," he answered querously, "but, come on now, all this was years ago and if no one complained then, why make a fuss about it now?"

"Then let me ask you another question," I replied, "if it's all so above board as it should be, why won't you let the kid Edward be crowned?" Richard rubbed his chin.

"I was hoping," he said, "to come to a proper understand with those Wydvilles. We can't go on like this, fighting about nothing..."

"The crown is nothing?"

"Of course the crown is everything," he almost spluttered, "but I don't see how we can start a new reign with the Wydvilles in one corner and the English nobility in another. You know how worried my brother was that this would happen. That's why he tried to bring us all together on his deathbed."

"Your brother was a fool," I said sniffily, "he should have known there were better ways of effecting a real reconciliation, if he wanted one. Don't kid yourself, he just wanted to die with a clear conscience." I sniggered. "But he didn't get away with it." Richard shook his head mournfully.

"And it was my fault for bringing up George's execution; after all, that was years ago. I shouldn't have done it. I blame myself entirely for how his life ended." I snorted.

"Don't waste any sleep over that guy, he wasn't worth it, sending his brother to the Tower and allowing his lady wife to sow discord anywhere and everywhere. And was he really into witches?" But Richard waved this away.

"I don't know. Perhaps. He was a superstitious sort of guy. As far as I'm concerned, it's all silliness."

"Well, Richard," I went back to our former conversation, "you have two choices – or rather about four. One. Crown Edward king. Two. If Edward really is illegitimate, there is Clarence's boy, another Edward, I think. Three. Let Henry Tudor, as the last Lancastrian heir and who's at least an adult, have the throne or ... "

"Or what?"

"Take it yourself." Richard got up. I thought he was going to leave in a funk but all he wanted was to top up his goblet. As he came back, he said:

"Both the Edwards are children and the problems that comes with one, comes with the other. If I crown Edward, the first one, we might have peace for six years while I am Lord Protector. But, still, I wouldn't count on the Wydvilles waiting that long to strike!"

"Further," I reminded him, "you might not live another six years." But this fell on deaf ears as Richard continued:

"As for Henry Tudor, that low born bastard, he will become king of England over my dead body." I shuddered. Prophetic words, indeed. He sighed as he sat down. "It's all about that damned greedy bitch, Elisabeth." I pursued my lips. Strong language. But Richard carried on: "She won't even talk to me; I've tried to see her I don't know how many times. Hiding herself behind sanctuary as if I were out for her blood. I thought by sparing her brother and that nasty son of hers when Buckingham had them locked up in Pomfret would bridge the gap between us, but obviously it has not."

"You could," I said dreamily, "keep Edward locked up in the Tower until he's 18, away from the Wydvilles." Richard glanced at me.

"Your ideas are getting more and more weird." But I had the last shot:

"A problem that has no solution is already solved." Richard frowned:

"And what do you mean by that?" I closed my eyes.

"Go figure."

I slept while Richard got on with his paperwork until one of the equerries, Jones, I think, came in:

"My Lord Protector, there are two Bishops here who wish to see you. They say you promised to assist them on a point of doctrine ..." Richard looked up, frowning:

"Doctrine? What on earth do I know of doctrine? Oh, well, they might as well come in. If I send them away, they'll only be back tomorrow." Richard got up and met the Bishops at the door. He took them to another part of the room while I nodded off but could still hear snippets of conversations.

"Ecclesiastics 10:16..."

"What's that got to do with anything?"

"The Bible itself is clear: *woe to thee, O land, when thy king is a child and thy princes eat in the morning.*"

"Don't we all break our fast in the morning"

"And the verse goes on: *blessed art thou, O land, when thy king is the son of nobles who eat in due season, for strength and not for drunkenness.*"

"That's all very well...what it is now?" He turned. Jones was back.

"Milord, the Duke of Buckingham and diverse gentlemen are here to see you. They are in the garden." Richard answered in irritation:

"Can't you see I'm busy? I've got to get rid of these two first. Tell the Duke and the gentlemen to come back tomorrow or, better still, a week from Wednesday." Jones scuttled away. Richard went on:

"I wish the Bible would be more straightforward. It gives me a headache trying to figure out what it all means." The Bishops persisted:

"My Lord Protector, the meaning is clear: a child will be a weak ruler..." Richard scratched his chin and said in a meditative way:

"...yes, and the nobles will go on a rampage." The Bishops nodded eagerly:

"Exactly, and so well spoken. A kingdom needs a strong ruler, from a noble lineage, not a child with doubtful antecedents." Richard was starting to tear out his hair.

But I got distracted from the learned discussion of Ecclesiastics by the tramp of many feet and a loud voice below my window. From its smarminess, I had no doubt to whom it belonged to: my lord, the Duke of Buckingham, who stopped right under my window and addressed the crowd:

"My Lord Mayor and citizens. Welcome. But I fear we may be on a bootless errand since the Lord Protector is within on business that cannot be interrupted. Ahh, here comes Catesby, his equerry. So, Catesby, what says my Lord?" I picked up my ears. This was curious indeed since Catesby hadn't been in to see Richard at all. I pushed open the window a tad wider so I could hear better and see, too. Catesby answered.

"I do apologize, my lord Duke, but the Lord Protector begs that you return next week as he is within with two Bishops, divinely bent on meditation. He says no worldly suit will draw him from his holy exercises."

Oh, ho, thinks I. These guys have got spin down to a fine art. However, I asked myself: was Richard in on the game or was it a ploy thought up by Buckingham and his gang? Buckingham boomed:

"Now, my good Catesby, please return and tell your master that I myself, the mayor and the good citizens of London have come to discuss with him a matter of great importance that will not wait. Tell him that we would not disturb him at such a moment if it were not imperative for the general good of the realm." Catesby left and Buckingham turned to the others and continued:

"You see, gentlemen, this prince is not like the late Edward, dallying with the ladies or sleeping it off, as they say." His laughter boomed. Titters were heard here and there. "Instead, he is at prayer for the enrichment of his soul. Happy would England be if this gracious prince were to become our King." A little silence. Then: "But I fear we shall not be able to convince him. He is too good, too loyal, too true." Someone spoke up, a tremor in the voice:

"Oh, dear, I do hope he doesn't turn us down."

This time Catesby actually came into the room. Richard turned to him, his irritation visible:

"Yes, what it is now?"

"My Lord of Buckingham is without with the Mayor and other citizens and would have some words with your Lordship. They swear not to leave until they have had audience with your Grace." Suddenly, Richard rubbed his hands and I could read his thoughts: this is how I get rid of these tiresome Bishops.

"No peace for the wicked," he said genially to his visitors. "I will myself show you out and see what is afoot." He placed a hand on the back of each prelate and almost pushed them through the door. I turned around and stuck my head out of the window so as to get a good look at what was coming.

As Richard stepped into the garden with the Bishops, the Lord Mayor said in awe:

"See, how he stands between two clerics holding Bibles!" Buckingham added sanctimoniously:

"Two props of virtue for a Christian king, to ensure that he stray not into vanity." In the meantime, Richard called Catesby over:

"My good Catesby, will you show these two worthy and holy gentlemen the way out?" and stood waving them genially on their way. However, they didn't leave but stayed half-hidden at the back of the crowd. Richard turned to the assembled mob, bowed slightly and said:

"Welcome, welcome all. There is no greater honour than to have English citizens call upon me. And my noble cousin, Buckingham," he bowed to Buckingham, "and my Lord of Norfolk," more bowing. "But pray tell me, what can I do for you all?" Buckingham of course was the spokesperson:

"My humblest apologies for having interrupted your devotions; such Christian zeal deserves all our respect." Richard looked puzzled and I was afraid he was going to say he didn't know all that much about devotions but what he did know was sufficient for his needs. Instead he chose to say:

"There is no business more important than that which concerns our citizens and the realm." He waited for Buckingham to go on.

"We have come," quoth that gentlemen, "on behalf of all good men in this ungoverned isle." Richard looked around nervously:

"I am afraid I have committed some offence and that you have all come here to chastise me for my fault." Buckingham lifted his arms to heaven.

"Indeed you are at fault, my Lord, and we are gathered here to ask you to amend it." Richard had that look he always had when he didn't really know what was going on. He took the safest path he could:

"And so I shall, if it be within my power to do so. But enlighten me as to what my error has been." I could have told him and saved him a lot of grief but I was too far away. So Buckingham said what all men knew but he, Richard.

"Your Grace, you have committed the fault of refusing the supreme seat, the throne majestical, the sceptered office of your ancestors; your due by birth, and for the unbroken lineal glory of your royal house." Richard eyes opened wide:

"I thought we'd already discussed this ..." but got no further before Buckingham went on, riding, so to speak, roughshod over Richard.

"You are leaving the throne of England to royal stock grafted and blemished with ignoble plants. We all heartily solicit you to take charge of this realm, not as protector, steward or substitute, but as successor, from blood to blood, your right of birth, your own. And so we have come, myself, these noble gentlemen and worthy citizens to move your grace in this just suite."

Of course, Richard should have expected this but I had to admire Buckingham; if he'd come alone, Richard would have slung him out on his ear. With this crowd milling around, it was much more difficult to wiggle out or take a rain check. He picked up the pieces, so to speak, as best he could and did a little squirming, then seemed to find his stride:

"I don't know whether to leave in silence or bitterly reproach you or your presumption. Although still of tender years, our prince, true son of my brother Edward, may in time become a good and conscientious king. On him I lay what you would lay on me, his rightful inheritance that I would not take from him." Buckingham looked pleased as punch. His arms flew out and he said with the biggest and falsest smile I had yet seen.

"My noble Prince, my beloved cousin, that is exactly what I would expect you to say and it argues to your grace's high moral and ethical standards. But, you, my Lord, as many others, unfortunately, remember only too well the kind of man your brother, the late king Edward of blessed memory, was. How he admired female beauty and how often he loved, yes, loved and promised marriage and more often than not did so by contract, which you know is as binding as a marriage itself.

"My Lady Elisabeth Wydville was one in this long line. You will admit, in consequence, among all these ladies the blessed Edward made promises to, Elisabeth's claim as his wife and queen was disputed at the time by the Earl of Warwick, a noble and worthy gentleman, and resulted in king Edward's exile." Richard opened his mouth to say something but Buckingham went on: "How can it be that the issue from such a doubtful alliance should inherit our realm, our England? No, no. The English royal house has only one true descendent and heir." The Lord Mayor added his bit:

"You must not refuse your subjects, good my Lord, I entreat you." Catesby added:

"Oh, make the people of England joyful, my lord, by granting this, their lawful suit." Richard glared at Catesby who wisely disappeared into the throng. There was a lot of noise now and Richard held up his hands asking for silence:

"My good people, believe me, I am unfit for state and majesty. Would you enforce upon me a world of care?" Norfolk now spoke up:

"My Lord, were there any alternative, any alternative at all, we would not ask you to take on such a burden. But there is none the Commons will accept. Do not cast our land into another civil war. This burden is placed on you by God himself and you cannot refuse."

Richard looked around desperately, saw me in the window and his eyes begged silent advice. I raised my shoulders and eyebrows and spread my paws out. Don't ask me, I'm only a cat. Seeing himself trapped, Richard submitted:

"My good friends, since you insist that I take up this heavy load, I suppose I must do so. God only knows how far I am from wanting this honor." Buckingham kneeled and so did everyone else. Richard cringed and Buckingham said merrily:

"Then I salute you with this kingly title: long live Richard, king of England." The whole crowd then shouted:

"Long live Richard, king of England!" Richard looked awful. He was obviously at the end of his rope and said in a pleading voice:

"Go now, my worthies, God's speed and may we meet again soon, gentle friends."

Richard came steaming into the chamber, threw whatever equerries were around out, called one back to get him strong wine and cast himself into a chair.

"I'm trapped, Gaius, trapped. What the hell am I going to do?" I sniggered.

"Indeed, good your Majesty, our Duke played upon you like a lute." He threw a shoe at me. "But, seriously, Richard, at the moment there was nothing to do but accept. I suppose you can always get out of it later, emigrate to the New World or something."

"What New World?" Oops, faux pas. I tried to correct myself.

"Well, there's bound to be one around somewhere." But Richard wasn't listening.

"Don't believe for a second that Buckingham wants me to be king except to further his own nepherous plots and stratagems, amassing treasure and power for himself and his acolytes. And he thinks, as he has acted the kingmaker, he can get whatever he wants from me. Well, I've got a new think for him. Not one penny-farthing or spoonful of earth will he get from me." He jumped up, came over to me and waved his finger in my face.

"And put this in your memory box, Gaius, I will not go to war again, not for anything. I'm sick and tired of fighting battles for others' gain and profit."

"But this time," I answered, "it would be for yourself." But Richard stood up tall and slapped himself on the chest:

"No, Gaius, I am condemned, I know I am. Those Wydvilles will rise up against me – and, let's be honest, who could blame them?" I jumped down from my window ledge and up on the arm of his chair. I put on my most earnest expression:

"Now, listen, Richard, and hear me well. While you have those two kids in the Tower no one, but no one, is going to mess with you. So keep them safe, my friend, for they are your security." Richard buried his face in his hands.

"Those poor kids, mere pawns in these suicidal grown-up games. I wish I could just let them go to live somewhere quiet."

"Well, you can't, Richard. Either you make Edward king or you become king yourself and keep Edward – and Richard – locked up." He answered mournfully.

"Well, Buckingham seems to have made up my mind for me. But what do we do about Edward?"

Unfortunately, the answer to that was not long in coming.

7

Interlude – Tea ... and sympathy?

F ar away, in Brittany, Lady Margaret Beaufort looked up from her knitting and peeked over her half-moon glasses.

"Henry," she said in a severe tone: "If I have told you once, I have told you a hundred times. Don't slouch. If you want to be king, you need to start behaving like one." Henry snorted but moved himself into a slightly less awkward but also less comfortable position.

"King," he sneered, "what hope in hell have I of being king?" Lady Margaret's needles clicked in a menacing sort of way.

"Now, Henry, we've been over this a million times. You are the last Lancastrian heir." Henry interrupted her rudely:

"Yeah, and don't say where there's a will there's a way. That bitch Elisabeth Wydville had about ten kids. Confounded fertile woman. Shall I perform a magic trick and, poof, they're all gone? To say nothing of dear King Richard. What kind of a cataclysm will it take to remove him?" Lady Margaret's needles clicked ominously.

"Henry, sulking won't make any of it happen. And grouching and complaining won't make the throne fall into your lap either. Now, go away and spruce up a bit; comb you hair, wash your hands and so on. We have visitors for tea."

"Oh, great," was the reply from Henry's back as he left the room. "The bloody Bishop again I'll be bound." He came back a few minutes later and was sitting down just as the maid announced:

"Earl Rivers et Lord Grey, Madam."

"Merci, ma cher Marie. Faite-les entrer, s'il vous plait." Henry stared at his mother.

"What on earth," he almost spat out, "are those two doing here?"

"Henry, my dear, if I have said it once, I have said it a million times. Don't be so impatient. And I know what they want and so would you if you used the brains God has given you." Rivers and Grey walked into the room. After their near death experience at Pomfret, they looked a lot less cocky; in fact, their manner might be called reserved and, at that moment, both seemed ill at ease.

"Lady Beaufort," said Earl Rivers with a low bow, "it is so kind of you to receive us." Lady Margaret smiled.

"Not at all," she replied, "Henry and I lead such secluded lives here that we enjoy visitors. Do sit down. Henry, will you move so that Earl Rivers and Lord Grey can sit on the Davenport? So comfortable, my late husband used to say. No, Henry, I would not move the cat. He has such an uncertain temper. Now, there, we are all comfortable. And here is Marie with the tea tray. Earl Rivers, milk or lemon? One lump or two? Lord Grey? And Henry, my dear, I know exactly what you like. There now, isn't this cosy?" Silence reigned while each concentrated on drinking tea. Then Henry asked:

"What news from our island nation?" Earl Rivers sighed.

"Not good, I'm afraid. The people groan under the yoke of Richard of Gloucester."

"You mean King Richard?" Rivers went scarlet.

"Never," he said through clenched teeth, "shall I give that monster the sacred title which belongs to my dear little nephew, may God bless him." Lady Margaret raised her eyebrows:

"Still in the Tower, is he?" Lord Grey sighed.

"Yes, and he has been joined there by his brother, Richard." Mother and son exchanged glances. "My mother," explained Lord Grey hastily, "thought it would be better for the boys to be together; at least they have each other."

"Like the time you took in two kittens, Mother, as you thought one might feel lonely." Lady Margaret glared at Henry.

"So like a mother," she answered soothingly, "to consider the welfare of her children above all else. How she must miss the lads." She sighed heavily and her voice took on a more tender tone. "The Tower. Well, I should not be happy if my small sons were locked up in that damp and gloomy place with Richard as gaoler." For a moment, a tear ran down her cheek. But then she rallied. "But still, a mother's heart knows best, and I'm sure Richard is a great comfort to Edward. A pity, though, that Gloucester should be holding both Yorkist heirs. And your mother remains in sanctuary at Westminster Abbey?"

Lord Grey nodded. "And I take it she gave up Richard to, well, Richard, from there?" Another nod. Lady Margaret sighed deeply. "Such a tragedy. It almost doesn't bear thinking of. Those lambs. Those poor lost lambs." There was silence for a bit. Then Lady Margaret continued:

"Now, it is not, don't think for a minute, my dear Earl Rivers and my dear Lord Grey, that we are not happy to see you but I must admit I don't believe you made the trip across the channel – was it rough? – for the pleasure of a cup of tea." Earl Rivers coughed into his handkerchief.

"Well, as a matter of fact," he admitted, "we do have a proposition to make to you since we are, shall we say, all in the same boat."

"And what boat might that be?" asked Lady Margaret in all innocence.

Henry snapped:

"The boat of state, mother, that will land either York or Lancaster on the throne of England." Lady Margaret raised her eyebrows.

"Indeed, how clever you are, my son. But there is no need to be so abrupt." She looked expectantly at Earl Rivers who said:

"Well, Ma'am, our objectives are the same, are they not. To rid England of Gloucester, the usurper." Mother and son exchanged further glances. This time Henry answered:

"It is clear that until we have managed to do so we are, as the saying goes, up the creek without a paddle."

"Therefore," continued Earl Rivers, "the Yorkist faction in England believe it would be in everyone's best interest if we made a compact with Lancaster; a marriage, my Lord Duke, between yourself and the Lady Elizabeth of York, eldest daughter of Edward IV of blessed memory." Lady Margaret replied with enthusiasm:

"Now there is a most charming idea, don't you agree, Henry? I am told Elizabeth is a most beautiful, accomplished and virtuous girl. The perfect wife for my Henry, to be sure. I've said so often enough, haven't I, my dear? It's time for you to settle down and become a family man. Wife, babes and the lot. Oh, I shall love being a grandmother! Perhaps a manor house in the country and you could go fox hunting or even be master of the hunt. Such a noble pursuit for a young man of good family." Henry intervened again:

"So you are proposing that my forces join yours, and that I cross the channel and together we make war on Gloucester?" Lord Grey nodded eagerly.

"Exactly so, my Lord. How well you have put it." Henry rubbed his chin with a finger.

"If we lose, of course, there is no doubt that Richard will have me killed. You also, my friends, although I am the greater prize. The last Lancastrian heir." Lady Margaret trilled with laughter.

"You must not be so pessimistic, my boy. I know what a great warrior you are. There will be a great victory and poor Gloucester will be utterly cast down. And you would marry Elizabeth right away and we would all go to London for Edward V's coronation. Cucumber sandwich, anyone?" She held out a plate. There was a silence that could be cut with a knife. Rivers and Grey exchanged covert glances, Lady Margaret knitted away and Henry looked out into the garden. Then Henry looked back at his guests.

"Yes," he said slowly, "that's the catch, isn't it? I would risk life and limb to put Edward V on the throne. And how would that be in my best interest?" Lady Margaret cut in:

"Come, come, now, my boy, you will be serving your country and your king. Isn't that a sufficient reward in itself? After all, we are too aware that while those sweet boys live – and may God preserve them for many many years – you will not be king, where you ever so much married to the sweet Elizabeth. A darling girl, to be sure. Such a tragedy, I think, this quarrel within families who should love and support each other. Do have a potted meat sandwich, Lord Grey." After a pause, Henry started again:

"You see, my friends. I am the Lancastrian heir; the sweet boys, as my mother puts it, are the Yorkist heirs. We cannot all be king, and one needs give way to the other. Would the Yorkists be willing to set aside the boys' right to the succession and let it pass to Elisabeth, their sister?"

"Oh, dear," exclaimed Lady Margaret. "It doesn't bear thinking of, taking the birthright away from the darling boys! But still, the

Bible does emphatically state: *Unhappy the kingdom that is ruled by a child.* So many wicked ambitious grown-ups around a poor innocent boy." Lady Margaret's needles cliked in a menacing way and there was now a steely look in her eyes as she looked from Rivers to Grey. "So, who knows, it might be for the best if they were no longer in the line of succession. Then Henry and Elizabeth would become King and Queen and all would be settled in the best possible fashion." Earl Rivers blanched:

"I am afraid I would not go that far, Lady Margaret. I do not think my sister the Queen would consent." Lady Margaret sighed:

"What a pity, it would seem such a perfect solution. A Win-Win situation, don't you think?" Another silence followed and Earl Rivers started to look desperate perhaps to get away from all that was not being said. Lady Margaret said. "Well, there we are. The boys, as dear as they are, are an obstacle to an alliance between us," she continued, "As we stand now, Lancaster and York have no common ground and each must pursue their separate ways towards a common goal that only one can reach." Rivers gasped:

"Madam, are you suggesting..." Lady Margaret bent over her knitting and said sweetly:

"I am suggesting nothing, Earl Rivers. Please do not put words into my mouth. So unbecoming of a gentleman." Rivers stood up and Grey hastily followed suite. Both bowed to mother and son and Lord Rivers said:

"This has been a most pleasant meeting, Lady Beaufort, and my Lord Duke. And so instructive." Henry also rose to his feet and bowed. Rivers continued: "I'm afraid we must leave now if we are to catch the tide." Lady Margaret said:

"Please give my best love to your sister, Earl Rivers, and tell her how I feel for her in her distress. If there is anything, anything at all, I can do for her she only needs to let me know. So brave with so much against her."

Earl Rivers and Lord Grey walked somberly down the drive towards their coach. Grey said:

"Did you understand, uncle, what I did?" Rivers nodded,

"It was as clear as clear, nephew; while those boys live we are all stuck with Gloucester as king. Good point, too. Damn Gloucester. He holds all the cards. Damn my sister, how could she be so stupid as to give both boys into Gloucester's keeping?"

Back in the drawing room, Henry looked out after the disappearing figures.

"Well, mother, we are no further."

"Nonsense, dear, we have come a long long way. Take my word for it, we will hear from them again."

Henry stretched himself out on the sofa.

"I cannot be king," he said glumily, "if I don't marry that girl, you know. And convince everybody I am ruling in her place as she is the true queen." Margaret shook her head.

"Dear Henry, a woman cannot inherit in England as you well know. But I agree with you – no Elizabeth, no throne." Henry scratched his nose.

"All this is very complicated," he answered "even if Edward IV's two boys were out of the way, the true king would be Clarence's kid, whatsit!"

"Another brat!" Lady Margaret shook her head. "I don't think England could put up with another boy king. The recent past is strewn with them – Richard II, Henry VI and now the glittering choice of another three." Her needles clicked. "Given a choice, I think it will be Elizabeth – and you."

8

Richard III

8.1 Coronation

The day of the coronation dawned bright and sunny, not a cloud in the sky. I know it was June 26th and it was supposed to be summer but, still, this was England where it rains regularly, regardless of the season. Richard and I were at Baynard's Castle from where he would set out for his coronation as had his brother, Edward, of unblessed memory, before him. I was lying on a window embrasure as usual, enjoying the sun, when Richard came in, all resplendent in his coronation finery minus, of course, the crown.

"Are you sure you won't come?" he asked. "I'll get you an ermine cloak and a small crown like those all the nobles put on when the king is crowned." I yawned.

"Sorry, pal, I'm not into cloaks, ermine or otherwise, and, as for crowns, my ears would get in the way." Richard twiddled his thumbs.

"I don't suppose," he said diffidently, "that you could stay in the Tower with the boys?" But here I was adamant.

"No! Those kids are your responsibility, not mine. It would be too depressing." Richard sighed.

"You're right, of course. But they won't know what's going on, anyhow, will they?" I sneered. Richard could be so dense. I said:

"How could they know? All London's church bells will be ringing and the cannons of the Tower will probably fire a 21-gun salute in your honour." Richard looked cowed.

"Gaius, I tell you, I don't think I should have taken this on." I settled myself down, after washing my face:

"Too late for that now. Off you go." At that moment, Anne, soon-to-be-Queen, came in looking really resplendent – she was, after all, a good looking woman, with the soon-to-be Prince of Wales, Eddie, a stripling of about six, by the hand. She sighed, too. This was a great day for sighs.

"I suppose we'd better go, my Lord," she said in a melancholy voice. There was a pregnant silence. She continued sadly: "I don't suppose we could just tell the carriage to drive north and go home? Let Edward be king." Edward, the soon-to-be prince of Wales, gave her a frightened look:

"Mama, I don't want to be king. I don't even want to be prince of Wales. Can't I stay here and play with Gaius?" I shook my head.

"That's the difference, kid, between being human and animal. Humans have to do as they are told. Animals just don't have to be caught." Richard also shook his head.

"My darlings, it's too late in the day. Let's face the music. At least we'll have done our duty." Anne said in a low voice:

"I have a bad feeling about all this." Her and me both. Looking like a three-some headed for Tower green and the scaffold, they left the room, heads bowed. I curled up and hummed:

> *"There may be trouble ahead*
> *But while there's music and moonlight and love and*
> *romance*
> *Let's face the music and dance.*
>
> *Before the fiddlers have fled*
> *Before they ask us to pay the bill and while we still have*
> *the chance*
> *Let's face the music and dance.*
>
> *Soon we'll be without the moon, humming a different*
> *tune and then*
> *There may be teardrops to shed*
> *So while there's moonlight and music and love and*
> *romance*
> *Let's face the music and dance!"* [6]

---

[6]   *Let's face the music and dance.* Irving Berlin (1888-1989)

Then I went to sleep.

I don't know how many hours had passed but it was already dark when I was awoken by angry voices shouting close at hand. The loudest and angriest I recognized at once. Buckingham, the Duke from Hell.

"You promised! You promised! You can't go back on our agreement now!"

"What agreement?" shouted Richard. "I know of no agreement."

"The earldom of Hereford, my ancestral lands, and your brother, king Edward IV, movables, once you were king." Richard went red in the face and turned on Buckingham like a tiger.

"Have you lost your wits? Why on earth should I give you anything – a finders' fee for getting me the crown? I became king at your instigation to protect what you called 'our ancient freedoms' which I take to mean license for you and your kind to continue to rob, plunder, pillage and wring both the crown and the peasants for as much as you can get.

"Well, I don't know where you got this idea, my friend and ally, but get rid of it. We will have no more 'giving', as you say, while I'm king. I don't have a 'giving' disposition. Have you forgetten Edward's gaggle of daughters? If I give you what you want, how will they get dowries and husbands? Or, for that matter, live. Shall I starve my own flesh and blood for your satisfaction?" Buckingham went scarlet in his turn.

"Edward's goods belong to the crown and the 'King' may dispose of them as the he sees fit." Richard turned away:

"Indeed. My dear Buckingham, I suggest you go through the courts for the earldom. Should be easy to prove it's yours, since you call it 'my ancestral heritage'. I may put in a good word for you with the judge. So, run along, now, there's a good lad. If you don't think you are rich enough, go find someone else to blackmail. On the other hand, I might give you a good price for poor Edward's movables if you're willing to pay. Make me an offer I can't refuse." Buckingham waved his finger in Richard's face.

"You will regret this! I made you and I can break you!"

"Oh, indeed. Well, knock yourself out, my friend and good luck to you." Buckingham stormed out. I stretched.

"Buckingham is no longer your bestest friend," I said, curling up.

"Good riddance," was the answer. Richard threw the crown down on a sofa and the rest of the coronation paraphernalia went on top of it. "I don't see why I should pay for something I didn't want."

"He will be a dangerous enemy."

"I don't care! And if you have nothing positive to say, I suggest you shut up." And so the conversation ended. Richard breezed off.

I decided I needed a walk and naturally found Buckingham sitting on the palace steps, his head in his hands. I was behind a great pillar, well hidden or so I thought, but then Buckingham spoke:

"Gaius, I know you are there!" I was surprised; Buckingham didn't usually speak to cats. But I kept my peace. "You know," he continued, "all this makes me think: why did all this happen? The civil war – for, no matter how you look at it, that's what is was." I growled deep in my throat just so he would know I was listening. He continued: "You may think, what about the getting of the garland, say, keeping it, losing and winning it again; it has cost more English blood than twice the winning of France." I heard a sigh in the dark. I answered:

"Too late for regrets, my friend! You and your kind should have thought of that before taking the chestnuts out of the fire for someone else's benefit." Deep silence. I continued: "I would think twice, if I were you, before going down that path again. Don't let that particular horseman ride!"[7] All lost because that was all the nobility – of any country – could think of. If you don't like your king, you impeach him and get another one. But, naturally some kings are stronger than others and object to being impeached. Hence, Civil War. I continued: "As kings go, you can do a lot worse than Richard." The voice came out of the dark.

"Really? Can't see how." Well, if he couldn't see there was no help for it. Lucky for Buckingham, he wouldn't live to see the result of his handiwork.

---

[7]   The Four Horsemen of the Apocalypse. Revalations.

It was way past Happy Hour when Richard came into the chamber where I was on my usual perch in the window embrasure. He threw himself down in the corner of a sofa, snapped his fingers and a menial came hurrying in with a goblet of wine.

"Bring the whole bloody bottle," snarled Richard, and the bottle materialized in a thrice.

"Well," I said smugly, "being king isn't so bad after all!" Richard growled.

"Believe me, it's the pits." I had a nice long stretch, back arched, sighed and lay down on my side, and went on:

"There's no one in this kingdom who wouldn't change places with you."

"There's no one in this bloody kingdom I wouldn't change places with," came the answer. He sighed. "To hold absolute power is for the birds." I started to say something but Richard interrupted me: "Yes, I know. *Power corrupts. And absolute power corrupts absolutely.*" In fact, absolute power drives you mad. He went on.

"Very clever, I'm sure, and oh so true." Silence. Then "Power is a frightening thing, Gaius. It's like a beast lying in wait, just ready to spring. Do you realize that if someone puts a paper in front of me, I ask what it is and can be told: 'new shoes for the kitchen staff', I might sign it only to find that in reality it's a warrant to execute Sir Thingummy. And as soon as I've signed, someone dashes off and before you can say 'Jack Robinson', the deed is done and Sir Thingummy is no more. But his effects are and, sure as eggs is eggs, someone's out there, just waiting to snap them up."

"It's a nasty world," I said in consolation. Richard shook his head in irritation.

"It's a nice world, with nasty human inhabitants." Couldn't argue with that. Richard continued:

"I keep having this dream where I sign a warrant of some sort only to find out it's for Anne's execution and I can't wake up and get it back." I said soothingly:

"Richard, I know you don't sign papers without reading them first since bitter experience has shown you what that can lead to." But Richard was the mood for self-flagellation:

"It scares the pants off me," he continued, "that I only have to give an order for someone to be sent to the Tower and off he goes. No one ever argues, no one ever says the guy needs to be tried in a court of law. I've tried having proper trials but the jurors keep looking at me anxiously, afraid they come up with the wrong verdict and are dragged off to prison in their turn."

"Well, Richard," I said patiently, "it's not surprising everyone wants to keep on your good side since your word is law." Richard got up and started pacing.

"But my word shouldn't be law!" he shouted. "The king should uphold the law, not trample all over it." I nodded sagely.

"Absolute power corrupts absolutely, but only if you let power become your master. If that happens, you are undone and so is everyone else around you until someone has the guts to assassinate you for the good of the realm. You need to understand and accept the fact that power isn't a Christmas present. It's been granted to you by those around you and will remain yours until you have pissed off enough people.

"You have power now, Richard, and you can use it either for good or evil. To gratify your every whim, your grandest dream. What is it you want? To conquer the world until you weep because there are no more worlds to conquer? To have all the jewels it's possible to possess and wear as many as you can at one time?" Richard shook his head impatiently:

"Of course not and you know it. And I don't like to be lectured by a cat." I ignored this last bit and went on:

"Then, why don't you use the power, while you have it, for something useful. Although they have forgotten it, kings are supposed to manage and administrate, but none of them do much of either because they think they have the power not to. So they dance about, carefree and gay, and distribute their power in dribs and drabs to underlings. Then they find it hard to take power back should they want to. Look at your history. Its full of good examples." I ruminated. "Of course, if the power is given to one man alone, you can always have him executed and the problem is solved." Richard looked at me reflectively:

"Perhaps, Gaius, you're not as cabbage headed as you look and there's something in what you say." He got up and threw on his cloak, upsetting the vine bottle standing on the floor. "I'm going for a walk to think it over. Oh, and get someone to come and clean up this mess." Power has its advantages.

Look back ... unto the Tower. Pity, you ancient stones,
those tender babes whom envy has immured within your walls -
rough cradle for such little pretty ones! Rude ragged nurse,
old sullen playfellow for tender princes - use my babies well!
So foolish sorrow bids your stones farewell

Richard III IV.1-2

9

Interlude at the Tower

I wasn't much for going out and about in London – the horrible streets covered in mud and muck, lots of fierce masterless dogs and nasty feral cats around with whom I had no wish to mingle, to say nothing of nasty little boys who would as soon bell a cat as eat a muffin. As for diseases – I am vaccinated myself but that is against 21st century bugs so I wasn't taking any chances. But one day I did wander around alone – why I have forgotten – in and around the Tower. I was sitting on a wall having a chat with one of the Tower ravens in a tree opposite when we heard sobbing beneath us. We looked down and saw a figure huddled by the Tower wall – a female all enveloped in a cloak of good quality.

"No beast so fierce but knows some touch of pity," she sighed. We looked at each other. The raven snikkerd:

"She must mean a lion that has just eaten." But the scene was too much for my curiosity and I jumped noiselessly down, approaching the woman from behind. She continued, her body racked with sobs.

"Oh, my little ones. I shall not see you again, hold you again; you will no longer know what it is to feel a mother's love," I heard her moan. "Did I bring you into this world for a fate such as this? Why didn't I marry a blacksmith; my children would have been safe and lived untroubled lives." Suddenly she looked around and saw me. And, of course, I recognized her at once. Ma Wydville. "You!" she screamed. "You, Richard's evil familiar!" and she threw a rock at me, just grazing my ear. Then something strange happened to me. I felt sorry for her. I know this is very uncat like, cats not having many emotions. But there it was. I was spending too much time with humans. I'd have to be careful or I'd end up losing my animal instincts and that is the quickest road to extinction. However, I went closer to her and said:

"Lady, do you want to see your kids?" Her tear streaked face looked at me in incomprehension.

"Kids?" she repeated.

"I mean your boys. If you do, I might be able to arrange it." Her nails scrapped the stone walls of the Tower. A horrible sound.

"See my boys," she repeated slowly, bowing her head. But then she jumped up and picked another stone – lots about, I'm afraid, and shied it at me. Luckily, her aim this time was off.

"No!" she screamed. "No! No! I don't want to see my boys!" She turned back to the Tower wall. She seemed to have forgotten me as she pressed hereself against the stones. "Pity, you ancient stones, those tender babes. Rude cradle for such little ones, old sullen playfellow!" Then she ran off like a demented fury. I sat there for a bit and thought about this strange scene. My friend the raven came down, perched next me and commented:

"That is one lady who has lost her marbles." I shook my head.

"Au contraire, mon cher ami," I answered. "That is one tough lady and, as you know, when the going gets rough, the tough get going. But there are limits. There are limits." The raven shook its head.

"Ambition," was its answer, "leads humans down strange paths."

10

Disaster strikes

10.1 Murder most Foul

I was dreaming. You can tell a cat is dreaming because its paws twitch, it makes cute little noises and its eyelids twitch. I was dreaming: masses of dark energy covered the sky, shifting this way and that like storm clouds; parting now and then and shwoing me glimpses of towers and battlements before obliterating the sky again. Then, all at once, it all vanished and I saw the Tower of London rearing up its ugly head, its black outline sinister against a stary sky. Then, dark energy returned, swirling and twirling around the four turrets. I woke with a start, my heart going like a pump. Something awful had either happened or was about to happen. I jumped up, down from the mantelpiece and onto Richard's bed, who was sleeping peacefully, snoring every so slightly. I started pummelling him as hard as I could.

"Richard," I shrieked, "wake up, wake up!" Richard tried to push me away, still half asleep.

"Damn cat," he said in a sleepy irritated voice. "Go away!"

"Richard," I screeched, "wake up, you've got to wake up! Something awful is going to happen or has happened at the Tower." That got his attention. He sat up, knocking me off the bed and onto the floor.

"What it is?" he cried, "is Whitehall on fire?" He jumped out of bed and started flaying about. "Where are my boots and my cloak? Where is my sword!" I scratched his arm to get his attention.

"Richard," I said, "you've got to stop fussing and calm down. We have to go to the Tower immediately!" He looked at me in a dazed way.

"The Tower? Is the Tower burning?"

"No, Richard, no," I cried with impatience. "But something is wrong there. Very wrong." He still looked blank.

"How do you know?" I jumped about, now fussing myself.

"Never mind how I know. We have to get there at once. At once, do you hear? At once and in secret." He was now fully awake.

"And why should I trust you? You may just have had a nightmare." Lord of cats, people irritate me sometimes – or rather, all the time. I scratched him again. He pulled his arm away, mopping the blood with the bed sheet.

"Will you stop that?" I looked at him in fury:

"If you don't trust my instincts, go right back to sleep. But on your head be it!" He looked at me, licking his wounds so to speak and then finally got going. He shouted for a valet of sorts. When the man came in, Richard told him to get a small boat – two oarsmen only and a watchman with a lantern – to be at the Whitehall pier in about two minutes.

"Go, go, go," cried Richard and the valet scuttled off. Now dressed, Richard sprang out of the bedroom and ran down the long hallway to the main palace entrance with me behind him, the guards along the route unmoving until the Sargeant came along:

"Sire..." he tried and got:

"Get out of my way," for his pains. "And don't let anyone know I've left. On your head be it if you do." The sergeant blanched. Richard ran at the same breakneck speed out onto the terrace, down the steps, into the garden, across the greensward and down the steps three at a time to the Thames dock. I could hardly keep up. A boat was waiting and he threw himself into it. I hesitated and considered letting him go on his own. This was not a gorgeous royal barge, decked with coloured lanterns, gold trimmings, pennants fluttering and 16 oarsmen on each side, music tootling under a bright sunny sky, but a dark skiff with two grubby-looking oarsman and a guy up front holding a lantern. I don't like boats or water at the best of times and this was not one of the best.

"Come on, damn you," roared Richard, and grabbed me by the scruff of my neck, something that hadn't happened to me since I last visited the vet. The boatman shoved off and the oarsmen pulled steadily downstream. It didn't take us long to see the Tower. There it loomed, huge and menacing, getting huger and more menacing the closer we got. Although I had been there before, the place never, as you might say, 'grew' on me and I found that each visit just made me dislike it more. And, of course, I had never seen it from the outside after dark. As in my dream, I could clearly see the outines of the massive walls and the four turrets rearing their ugly heads into the sky.

Then my dream returned in waking mode. The air around it swirled with darkness and the whole building seemed to disappear into a large black gaping hole. In my fright, I dug my nails into Richard's calf and he cursed me. Slowly, the Tower re-emerged in all its frightening massiveness. The oarsmen started pulling in.

"Traitors' gate," I screamed, recognizing the Romanesque arch and the nasty iron grills, "why are we going through the traitors' gate? What am I suspected of? Are you going to cut my head off?"

"I might," came the answer, "if you don't shut up." Then he relented and said:

"I really don't want all and sundry to know we're here. So we'll just slip in quietly."

He jumped onto the dock, climbed the steps, through the St Thomas Tower, the Bloody Tower and across the greensward into the White Tower. This brought us to the guardsroom; here, all was peace and the guards were taking it easy, boots off, weapons strewn around any old how. Those off duty were playing cards or it might have been tiddlywinks for all I knew, while those who were supposed to be on guard were hanging on their haldberds and giving the players advise, probably all bad. Helmets and breastplates were thrown around any old how and here and there were odds and ends of meals that a couple of dogs were fighting over. One showed me his yellow teeth; I hissed and arched my back but before a brawl could start, Richard snatched me up and flung me up the stairway leading to the west turret, sprinting up hard on my heels. As he stormed off, the guardsmen tried to get themselves together but Richard just shouted:

"As you were: I was never here." He literally flew up the stairs, leaving me absolutely nowhere. We reached the first landing and the royal apartments; a hallway stretched ahead of us but one door was open and Richard stormed straight through it. I hung back. I was starting to feel sick. Whatever I had felt in my dream had already happened. We were too late.

The air swirled with negative energy: fear and greed and cunning and despair. I considered facing the dogs downstairs as a suitable alternative to facing whatever was in the room beyond. Cowardly? If you say so. But *he who fights and runs away will live to fight another day*. Not that I would consider fighting – running away was more my line. But then Richard's voice barked out:

"Gaius!" I slunk in and jumped up on a low window sill, trying to make myself inconsuspicuous.

10.2 A third High Crime?

There were three men in the room: Sir Robert Brakenbury, lieutenant of the Tower, standing ramrod straight; Master William Slaughter, the princes' tutor, sitting in a chair, back bowed, his hands covering his face, shaking convulsively. The third was Sir James Tyrrel, most confidential of Richard's henchmen and whom he, Richard, trusted implicitly. Richard turned to Tyrrel:

"What's been going on here?" Without a word, Tyrrel pointed to the bed. And my eyes followed his pointing finger as did Richard's. The two boys, Edward and Richard, were lying on their backs side by side, in their nightshirts, heads close together, for all the world as if they were in a deep slumber, but covered by neither quilt nor blanket, both lying on the floor in a heap together with the pillows. The smell of death was unmistakable. Richard walked over to the bed and shook the oldest, Edward. Edward didn't respond. Slaughter's sobs increased in intensity. And then the penny dropped. With a horrified look on his face, Richard drew his hand back.

"Oh, my good Lord. Oh, sweet Jesus. He's cold!" he gasped, "why is he so cold?" He touched Richard, too, shaking him. "And this one, also. Why are they uncovered? Slaughter, come here and ..."

"They are dead," I said from my windowsill. Richard turned and looked at me wildly.

"How do you know? You haven't even looked at them properly."

"I can feel the energy in the room," I answered, "the children's fear and the murderer's purpose." Richard staggered backwards, his hand to his forehead.

"They can't be dead! Why should they be dead?" He went back to the bed, one hand on each boy's brow. And then he had to accept the awful truth. Both boys were dead.

"How can this be? Who found them?" cried Richard. Tyrell answered:

"I did, my Lord. When I saw what had happened, I summoned Sir Robert. Master Slaughter was not in the room but arrived at the same time as Sir Robert." Sir Robert said gravely:

"I closed their eyes, my Lord."

"Arrived?" gasped Richard, a step behind the various explanations. "Arrived from where? Slaughter, you were to watch over them at all times." Slaughter uncovered his tear stained face.

"Sire, I did, I did. I was only away for a few moments, I needed a new candle," he pointed over to a corner, to a chair, small table, an empty candleholder, with an unused candle on the floor. Tyrell sneered.

"A likely story, my lord," he said coldly, "it would take more than a few moments to smother both boys!"

"Smothered?" gasped Richard. "How do you know?" Tyrrel picked up one of the pillows.

"Look," he said, "here is the imprint of a face, drool and saliva. And look at their bodies. How else could they have died?" Richard sat down then jumped up and pointed his finger at the three men, one at a time:

"One of you, it must have been one of you!" Sir Robert bristled.

"Not so, my lord," he said firmly. "You ordered me to turn over the key to the entrance of the White Tower to Sir James Tyrrel, which I did. So, I have had no access to the princes and cannot therefore in any way be involved." Slaughter cried out between sobs:

"I was locked in with them. I loved them, I have been with them so long, they were so dear to me." His sobbing increased and I was afraid he would go into convulsions. Richard turned to Sir James Tyrrel.

"And what about you, sir?"

"My lord, I am your sworn bondsman. What reason would I have to carry out such a heinous act which I know is not in your interests?"

"I see," said Richard, "you're all as innocent as babes unborn. Get out, all of you, and leave me alone. Get out but don't leave this turret. And don't speak to anyone!" They scuttled off as fast as they could; there was certainly no standing on ceremony since Slaughter was first out the door.

That left Richard and me and the dead. It was now Richard's turn to bury his face in his hands.

"Oh, my poor little nephews. To have ended their short lives in such a way and in this place. And alone, Gaius, children alone with a killer!" He was silent for a while. "Well, Gaius, who was it? You should be able to recognize guilt since you claim you can feel everything else." I stretched, jumped down and onto the bed. I sat between the bodies. I touched them; quite cold. They must have been dead for some little time. I felt sad. Children's lives shouldn't end like this. In answer to Richard's query, I said somewhat distantly:

"Sorry, Richard, I am not a one-cat judge and jury and, anyway, it really doesn't matter who did it, does it?" He glared at me.

"And what do you mean by that, if I may ask?" I answered:

"Richard, whether it was one or the other, the boys are dead." Richard jumped up in a frenzy:

"I will throw the lot into the deepest dungeon," he shouted. "I will have them racked until their bones break! I will know who did this!" He stormed around the room.

"Richard! Richard!" I had to shout as loudly as a cat can to make him hear me. At last he stopped his mad ravings and looked at me. "Richard, it doesn't matter who killed them because, whoever did it, was merely an instrument. So, no rack or water boarding, thumb screws or whatever else you may have in your bag of tricks down in the basement." Richard wanted to argue:

"But I could get the name of whoever sent them – or him."

"And so what, Richard? We don't need anyone to tell us who it was. We can figure that out by ourselves. After all, the list of suspects is quite short." Richard sat down and looked at the floor:

"How can you be so callow? I thought you liked the kids. How can you see such a scene as this and not feel anything?" I moved to the foot of the bed.

"Richard, someone must keep his head or all is lost. And don't speak to me of my feelings; you know nothing about them." Richard shook his head:

"The boys are dead and they died on my watch. What more can be said?" He sighed and wiped tears away with the back of his hand.

"Richard," I said, "look at me. What do you intend to do?"

"Why, give them a proper Christian burial," he said, "what else is there to do?" I sneered:

"Right! Big ceremony in Westminster Abbey. Ma Wydville and her hundred daughters all dressed in black and weeping into lace handkerchiefs. The great unwashed, crowds upon crowds of them, shrieking and howling in sympathy with the grieving mother. Calling for a head ... a head ..." Richard got the point.

"They'll say I did it!" I sneered:

"Move to the head of the class." Richard had caught up with me:

"And they will raise a rebellion against me."

"You get a gold star," I said. "Do you want to be the cause of another Civil War? Because that's how it will end if we follow your scenario." Richard shook his head. I answered for him: "Done that, been there, bought the t-shirt, haven't you? Are you ready for another round?" Richard shook his head:

"No, I certainly am not. But I don't see how it can be avoided once this gets out."

"Well," I said, "let's make sure it doesn't for as long as possible. Time is a precious gift, the more time one has, the more one can influence the future. Give yourself that time and maybe, maybe, a way out can be found." I got a quizzical look:

"Do you believe that?" I didn't, of course, not totally but I felt it was worth a shot. Richard picked up a coverlet and laid it over the two corpses.

"What a mess," he groaned. "What a mess! So what do you suggest we do now?" I answered:

"We keep this quiet for as long as we can." Richard stared:

"You mean..?"

"I do," was my reply.

Slaughter, Sir Robert and Sir James were back in the room. Richard made them sit down and walked up and down in front of them.

"Gentlemen, I cannot tell you how much this tragedy has affected me. The princes are dead, they were my nephews and I loved them. How they died and by whose hand is irrelevant to us. What we need to do is to keep their deaths a secret. No one outside this room must know. You, Slaughter, I want you to continue living here, getting in food, bathwater, laundry, whatever, changing sheets, bath towels and so on. No one else will enter these rooms." I held up a paw.

"Richard, the room should be cleaned once a week by a maid, while Slaughter takes the boys into the garden."

"Well remembered, Gaius. Right as usual." Slaughter whined.

"But what am I going to do with all that food? I'm a very picky eater."

"That," said Richard, "is your problem. Get a dog or two. You, Sir Robert, will continue on your usual rounds. If anyone asks about the boys, they are doing well but cannot receive visitors. But that's business as usual. And, Tyrrel, you will continue coming to the Tower about once a week as you have been doing to check on things and so on. The three of you can take tea together – or have a drink. I don't care!" Richard paced some more. "Now, gentlemen, and I can't stress this point enough. No one must know the boys are dead. And I mean: no one. Don't tell your wife, your mother, don't whisper it to your mistress, boyfriend, best drinking buddy. If I hear one whiff of a rumour doing the rounds, whether among the gentry or the hoi polloi, the three of you will breathe your last that day. Do I make myself clear." Three heads nodded. Sir Robert said in a small voice:

"What is to happen to the bodies?"

"Unfortunately," replied Richard, "we cannot give them a Christian burial, much as I would like to. No priests, no service." He looked downcast. "The boys must be buried somewhere within the Tower. Some out of the way nook where no one ever goes." He scratched his head. "Perhaps we can have them moved later to some more dignified grave."

"I know just the place," sighed Sir Robert, "under the stairs in the East wing, you know, Sir James, as you walk down to the dungeons."

"Thank you, Sir Robert," and Richard patted him on the back. "So, boys, let's get on with it, shall we?" And they did, taking the bodies not down the main stairs which would mean passing through the guardsroom but by a secret narrow passage that led in the opposite direction. I sat guard at the top of the stairs to make sure no one came up. What I would have done if anyone had, I really don't know.

10.3 Cui Bono?

When we got back to Westminster, Richard threw himself on the bed and I jumped onto my window embrasure. For a moment, silence reigned until a servitor of sorts came running in with a jug of wine, a mug and some water for me. Richard waved his hands:

"OK, thanks and get lost." The servitor scampered off. Richard filled his mug to the brim and drank it all down in one go. "Well," he said with a sigh, "that certainly cooks my goose." I cocked an ear. I had a wee stretch, licked my paws clean. Richard continued: "I may be as innocent of those terrible murders as a babe unborn, white as the driven snow but, as sure as eggs is eggs, I shall get the blame." I considered:

"Really, Richard, I don't see how. The question will only come up if the bodies are found, which seems unlikely." As if he hadn't heard me, Richard went on:

"You keep saying it doesn't matter who killed them but I just can't buy that. Of course it matters." I sighed again. Honestly!

"The trouble is, Richard, you are looking at the wrong scenario. You think of murder and consider either Sir James, poor old Slaughter or Sir Robert for the part of murderer. Of course you're right - basically; one of those three held pillows over those boys' faces and smothered them. But let me ask you something: you must have heard of the great Roman orator advocate and politician, Caius Tullius Cicero, who lived at the time of Julius Caesar." Richard refilled his mug.

"I've heard of Julius Caesar," was his disinterested answer.

"Well," I said, "Cicero set a legal precedent which became the keystone in all future murder investigations." Richard sighed so deeply and so long I never thought he'd never finish; then his weary comment was:

"Well, Gaius, and what are you driving at?"

"Cicero," I continued, "in his first big case as a defense attorney asked: *'Cui bono'*, which, in case you don't remember your Latin, means *to whose benefit*?"

Richard's brow was turning black and I could see he was looking for something to throw, so I hurried on:

"Cicero claimed that his client was innocent because he, the client, did not benefit from the death of the victim but that there were others who did." A boot flew in my direction; as usual, Richard's aim was lousy.

"Gaius, sometimes you are really insufferable. What on earth are you nattering on about?" I sighed. Richard was a nice guy but somewhat intellectually challenged. "If you have something to say, will you please get on with it!"

"Richard," I said, "I am thinking of those two dead kids in the Tower. For all our theorizing about who did what, we need to consider *who benefited* from their deaths – *cui bono*, in fact." Richard ground his teeth:

"Can you honestly tell me, Gaius, that you think I don't benefit?" Really, people are so dim. "Putative suspects, no matter what you say, are thin on the ground."

"Tell me, Richard," I asked, putting my head on my paws, "how would you benefit from the boys' deaths?"

"It's obvious, my dear Gaius, I would have eliminated the two main challengers to my right to the throne." I laughed silently and stroked my whiskers.

"And how do you figure that? The kids Edward and Richard were declared illegitimate, the English nobility accepted that as fact, so to speak, and you have been crowned king."

"Still, those kids would always remind people that I am a usurper."

"Richard, you are not thinking. The place is crawling with heirs to Edward IV – that Elisabeth had more kids than I have claws. First, by killing the boys, you would declare the story of the illegitimacy to be a lie – and yourself to be a usurper. That puts Edward IV's kids right back in the line of succession. You must agree that it would be a very stupid thing to do." Richard countered:

"Those kids died on my watch, Gaius. That Tower is just about impregnable – who else had access but myself and my henchmen? You just can't get around that I had motive, means and opportunity. Who else could it be?" I jutted out my jaw – such as it was – and replied:

"I still hold that your best strategy was to have kept those kids alive – in the Tower. You had means and opportunity but you had motive only if you'd taken leave of your senses. Anyway, who's going to accuse you?" Richard started pacing, always a bad sign. After a few turns around the room, he said:

"Gaius, someone must know the kids are dead. I don't mean the three guys we just saw. I am positive they won't speak." That's my Richard, such a trusting soul. "So what's to keep this person – or persons – from declaring the kids dead and accusing me of murder?" I sighed and crossed my paws in front of me:

"Richard, it's obvious someone knows – in fact, I think quite a lot of people know – but here's the rub – how can anyone come forward and accuse you? At the first hint, you would bung our three friends into the Tower and wring a confession out of one of them – or all three, for that matter. No, Richard, that is not the way it'll go. It's far too dangerous. It raises questions such as: 'when did he – or she – know and how did he – or she – know it?' Believe you me, that ain't the way it's going to play."

"So, my clever puss, what's next in your investigation? As the Tower wasn't taken by storm, how did someone manage to kill the kids?" I waved this away with a disdainful paw:

"It may be virtually impossible to take the Tower from the outside but you can buy treachery within, my noble friend. One man can be bought – a man with access. Elementary, my dear Richard."

"So one of the three guys there – Slaughter, Sir Robert or Sir James – sold out and murdered those children. So what are we going to do about it?" Really, when humans get obtuse, I just want to cry. It takes such a lot of explaining.

"Richard," I said, "if I stick a knife in you, who do you blame? The knife? The knife is only an instrument; if I wanted to murder you, a baseball bat or a dose of arsenic would do as well. Thus, the instrument used is immaterial." He glared:

"Are you saying it doesn't matter which of the three did the deed?" Lord of cats, give me patience. I answered:

"Oh, I have no doubt who did it – and I don't think you do either. Sir James is certainly the most likely candidate. He always was an unprincipled and greedy bastard. Slaughter is scared of his own shadow and Sir Robert is a man of honour – so to speak – he will support whoever is top dog." Richard scratched his chin.

"Sir James? Really, Gaius, I don't think so. Why, he looked me straight in the eye when he said he found the kids dead. He couldn't possibly have been lying." Oh, gimme a break!

"My dear Richard, an innocent man would not, as you say, 'have looked you straight in the eye'. He would have been frightened, afraid of being accussed and not able to defend himself. In fact, he would have behaved just like Slaughter did. The guilty man would be prepared, know the answers to the questions that would inevitably be asked. Like Sir James." Richard wrung his hands. Another bestest friend who had turned out not to be so bestest after all. Then he said:

"So what are we going to do about Sir James?"

"Nothing."

"What do you mean, nothing?" I sighed with impatience.

"Richard, we decided that your trump card to health, happiness and being king of England was to keep the kids locked away. So to accuse Sir James, you will have to admit that they are dead, which is not on your agenda. And, by the way, what possessed you to order Sir Robert to give Sir James the key?" Richard looked embarrassed as well he might.

"I have done so occasionally when I couldn't go to check on the boys myself."

"So you trusted Sir James implicitly."

"Noo, I can't say I did, but I did think he knew which side of his bread was buttered." I sighed:

"I see. But jam is also nice. Well, Richard, let this be a lesson to you when choosing whom to trust. I think Sir James is a scoundrel but I also think he does not come cheap. But what is done is done and we must move on as best we can." Richard turned his hands into fists:

"God, what a fool I have been. So Sir James was bought. And under my very nose. He benefits, financially." He pondered a bit. "But the ultimate prize is not whatever monies Sir James got but the crown of England and the power that goes with it and those are not within Sir James' reach, dead boys or not."

"And who's path might be smoothed to the throne by the death of those boys?" Richard did some more head scratching.

"The most probable candidate would be Henry Tudor, and his bona fides as a true and gentle knight cannot be said to be either impecable or above board." I nodded.

"Right! Henry is the logical suspect but he is tucked away in France – a long long way away – and somehow I don't think his arm reaches very far since we both know he's broke. Also, remember this: if we look once more at the illegitimacy of Edward IV's kids, we have to acknowledge that whoever challenges you for the throne must do by so supporting Edward's kids as the true claimants. That would not fit Tudor's book – if they were alive. Ergo: Henry: motive: in spades; means: none; opportunity: none. So who else is there?"

"Elizabeth of York," said Richard promptly, "although women can't inherit in England."

"True," I conceded, "but the throne can pass through a woman. So the best bet for anyone wanting to be king would be to marry Elizabeth."

"Which brings us back to Henry Tudor who is the only claimant of the right age." I tore my fur in despair.

"Great, Richard. Henry Tudor goes to Elizabeth and says: 'Ok, love, let's kill your brothers, get rid of Richard, you and I can be married, become king and queen and live happily ever after." Richard was starting to look irritated.

"Gaius, you're running around in circles. You say Henry Tudor didn't buy Sir James' services, and with your next breath that Henry will be the primary beneficiaty from the princes' deaths. You just can't have it both ways." I smirked and Richard threw a cushion at me that I pummeled carefully to get it just right and curled up on it.

"You, my friend, have missed a major player in this game who stands to gain, well, perhaps not the throne except in a vicarious way, but power. Perhaps even unlimited power: the Wydvilles." Richard gasped.

"Gaius, do you really believe Elisabeth Wydville would agree to the death of her own sons? It's repulsive." I examined my claws.

"Don't be obtuse, Richard, history and the tabloids are full of women who murder their children for much – and I mean much – less. And don't forget she wouldn't do it personally, but she must be an accessory both before and after the fact." Richard got up and floundered around the room, turning and twisting this way and that.

"But those kids were the Wydville's best way to power."

"Not while they were in the Tower. And don't forget, Richard, there are a lot of Wydvilles. Think of it like this: the Wydvilles are out of power; the real king and his immediate heir are in the hands of a powerful usurper king who, everyone wants to believe, has no scruples at all. Once they admit to themselves that the boys are lost as a way to the throne, what is their next step? Elisabeth is the next heir, but not while the boys live. They need a male claimant and Henry Tudor is the only game in town.

"But Henry won't budge until he knows the coast is clear, that Elisabeth is the heir, hence that the boys are no longer among the living. Ergo, the Wydvilles have no recourse but to get rid of the boys, no matter how much they love them and how many tears Ma Wydville has and will shed.

"The Wydvilles are in London, they have funds since they looted the Tower treasury, and they can get at Sir James easy enough. Motive: power; means: plenty; opportunity: difficult but not impossible. With Henry and Elizabeth on the throne, the Wydvilles are back in the great game." Richard sat down heavily.

"Well," he said, "I'll be damned." We were silent. Then Richard said:

"I need some air. I'm going for a walk." While I waited for him to come back, I thought of my meeting with Queen Elizabeth at the Tower wall but this I would not share with Richard.

When Richard came back and was getting ready for bed, I asked:

"Tell me something, Richard. If the Tower had been stormed, were your instructions that Sir Robert was to kill the boys?" There followed a silence that seemed to last a long time. The Richard said slowly:

"Well, no, Gaius, there weren't."

"Oh. I see. So if the Tower were taken, what would you have done?"

"To be honest, I don't know. But murdering my own flesh and blood – and children at that – was not on my list of priorities."

Richard snuffed out his candle and the room fell into darkness. "I thought I would cross that bridge when I came to it." After quite a long silence, I heard him mutter. "A mother agreeing to the murder of her sons! How unnatural. I still can't believe it."

Well, and who would? Greed makes strange bedfellows. In the future, Richard's back would be a bit more bent, and more cresses would appear about his eyes. I felt somewhat responsible since I was the one to have come up with such an unnatural and macabre solution. I won't apologize; I'm a cat and completely unsentimental. Though, I too, would never be the same cat I had been before.

11

Interlude in Brittany

Henry Tudor came riding up the path leading to the mansion lent to him by the Breton Prime Minister, Pierre Landis, his hunting companions some way behind him. His mother stood on the lowest step leading from the veranda down into the garden. She had sent a stable lad to get Henry back from hunting. When he reached the house, he jumped off his horse, throwing the reins to a boy who took it away. He faced Lady Margaret.

"Well, mother? And what is so urgent?" he asked although he knew, none better, that if his mother had called him back it was not only urgent but critical. Lady Margaret was holding a sheet of parchment, its seal broken. She handed it to her son. He read:

"Suffer the little children to come unto me"

That was all. Henry and Lady Margaret looked at each other. Lady Margaret was pale and quite unlike herself and Henry shivered. Henry said slowly:

"I suppose you could say we pushed them to it." Lady Margaret shook her head.

"No, Henry, their ambition pushed them to it." Henry said gloomily:

"This whole affair will come back to haunt me, I know it will." He walked into the mansion. "I'd better start packing."

12
Doubts and Questions

Following the death of the two princes, Richard was more than distraught. He walked around wringing his hands, blowing his nose and running his fingers through his hair. All right, the whole mess was awful but one must recognize when a problem is unsolvable! If there is no solution, the matter is solved! Have I said that before? Sorry!!

The worst was that he had gotten into the habit of picking me up like an old shoe and taking me either to the turret or to dungeons where he wanted to go discussing the matter endlessly. I had to keep fully awake during these session before in a fit of passion he might through me out of the window (from the turret) or forget me in the dungeon.

His most frequent question was:

"How can a mother do such a thing? I don't believe it, I really can't." This was very tiresome.

"Richard," I'd answer each time, "we've discussed this matter to death – sorry. Infanticide is not unknown in the world and probably happens a lot more often than anyone knows." Of course he wouldn't listen.

"She's their mother, Gaius, their mother! It goes against nature!"

"You obviously think Ma Wydville incapable of this deed," I would answer for the fifteenth time, "even considering the awful things she's been up to in the past." I stretched a bit; I was becoming stiff with all these conversations. "Look at your history!" Richard walked a bit more and flung his arms about some more.

"I know, I know!" I cut in.

"There the kid – whatshisname, "the son of Geoffrey and grandson of Henry II. He just sort of disappeared." But Richard wasn't buying.

"Gaius, that was done by a man. John Lackland, his uncle, not by his mother." I looked around for something to throw at him but all I could was an anvil (this time, we were in the dungeon) too heavy for a cat to lift. To I said for the twentieth.

"Richard, you seem to forget that she didn't have to do it herself, just to agree."

"A mother! A mother!" cried Richard wringing his hands until they were about worn out.

At the end, I had to become sharp with him. I dug my claws into his left thigh making him jump and yelp.

"Richard, if she didn't agree to it then you did it." He stared at me in horror. "Well," I sneered, "it's either one or the other. There is no third way no matter how popular the concept may be. He settled down for a bit and had a swig from the bottle he had the good sense to bring with him. Dutch courage! All men need it. We cats don't because we have our claws. I continued:

"Richard, you must get yourself together, you can't fall apart like this. You still have the run the kingdom. Or you could just up and walk away."

"Well," he scratched his head, "we both know I can't do that. But, boy, do I want to!"

"You've got Anne and little Edward to think of," I continued. "Don't let them down or throw them to the wolves."

He got up, picked me up and put me over his shoulder and we went to the world which was now so horribly changed.

This went quiet after that, no grand parties at the palace and Christmas, Twelfth Night and New Year could have been periods of mourning. A few visitors trickled in, but they were far between. And everyone who did come looked ascance at Richard, didn't really want to sit down in case they needed to beat a quick retreat.

I kept thinking of upping and going back home where things were very uncomplicated but I knew I wouldn't leave Richard at this moment of peril of his life. Even cats have a sort of loyalty or honor. Now, I now it was going to get much much worse but still I hung on. I was becoming very fond to Richard, to say nothing of Anne and Eddie.

13
Rebellion!

So, why wasn't anyone surprised when Richard's bestest friend Buckingham rose in rebellion against him? Buckingham lived his life on an emotional plain, buttressed by greed and gain, sort of 'I want it – and I want it now and I want more!' So if the Wydvilles had told him Richard had murdered the boys, he was their man to rise up and defend the innocent – for a share of the spoils and good old revenge; he had his own grudges against Richard so he and the Wydvilles now shared the same objective. RIG – Richard must go!

Very short sighted of Buckingham. All things being equal, Richard was the best king available whether at the short or medium term. OK, Richard tended to be aloof and largesse in the way of castles or counties or taxation rights or profitable monopolies didn't drip from his fingers. His was a new style of government. The court remianed very sober and parties were rare; when they did happen, there was no banqueting to all hours or rivers of wine or mountains of viands. I wouldn't say guests got 'today's special' but that was only because Richard hadn't thought of it.

On the other hand, he chopped off the minimum indispensible number of heads, didn't throw people into the Tower on a whim and wasn't interested in foreign wars. This left the nobility confused and many of them wanted to go back to the 'good ole days', having forgotten what the 'good ole days' had been like.

When he heard of his former pal's rebellion, Richard sighed, shook his head and went off to deal with him.

Here, I think I need to add that Richard had made an offer to M Landis, Prime Minister of Brittany, to, so to speak, 'buy' Henry Tudor for hard cold cash, and M Landis had been very tempted. Unfortunately, Henry heard about the deal, upped stakes and took off for Paris.

France was having troubles of its own with a minor on the throne, Charles VIII. The Regent, his sister Anne, was trying to deal with the Estates General who were not happy with a woman as Regent. Not surprising, considering French women only got the vote in 1947!

Foreign troubles are always popular in any country when things are not going well at home and the Regent Anne was happy to give Henry Tudor a couple of ships (probably quite unseaworthy) and some soldier she had no immediate use for, and Henry set off for England to join his former enemy, Buckingham.

To cut a long story short, the whole thing was a disaster. Not due to Richard's generalship or prowess in battlr but bad weather, the bane of those trying to cross the English channel. Henry's fleet, such as it was, was blown all over the place and lucky to get back to France instead of becoming food for fishes. Meanwhhile, the weather in England was appalling – as ususal.

Richard caught Buckingham when his troops abandoned him – they may have been ready to die for the cause but not in the rain.

When Richard got back to London after all this, he was in a bad mood. He threw his muddy boots at a servant and shouted for wine – and lots of it. Happy hour taken care of, he sighed. Richard had a lot to sigh about just then.

"Gaius, I never knew such a fellow for manipulating, scheming, plotting and conniving as our old friend Buckingham. Like a bull in a china shop. With him on the rampage, there's no safety for man or beast." More sighs. "I had to execute him, Gaius, he was a menace to one and all." He looked sadly at his hands. "Gaius, my hands are covered with blood; first, poor Hastings, who was ever my friend, and now Buckingham."

"Your friends," I sneered sardonically, "pardon me, but kings don't have any. They have sycophants who try to profit from being close to the throne. Will ye or nill ye, I'm afraid this method – Tower and execution – is the way England – and so many other countries – are governed." I stretched and rolled over on my other side: "Tell me, Richard, who else did Buckingham drag into this mess?" Richard sighed – again:

"Really, Gaius, I don't want to think about it. Buckingham seems to have convinced about ninety squires, knights or what have you to be join him." He laughed, not real laughter but the sardonic kind: "I wonder how many words they were allowed each during strategy meetings." He twiddled his thumbs. "Anyway, I had to impound their lands; rather sad, really, but I couldn't let this kind of behaviour pass." I pulled at my whiskers:

"No one else lost their head?" Richard shook his head.

"I find it a such a disgusting way of killing people." He shivered. "I mean, in theory the axe comes down and the head is severed. But it's not really that cut and dried." No pun intended, I am sure. "Some executioners are bad at their jobs and need ten strokes to get a head off.

"Others get drunk the night before and go to work with hangovers. I should not like to do that kind of work and perhaps they don't either. As for hanging, drawing and quartering, not while I'm alive." He shuddered. I wondered whether I should tell him about the guillotine – he would have loved that, it's so efficient; then there's the the gas chamber or a needle in the arm but I decided he wasn't ready for any of this. He went on: "Of course, the Countess of Richmond, Henry's fond mamma, was in it but I limited myself to turning her property over to her husband, Lord Stanley. As for the Duchess of Buckingham, being married to the late lamented seemed to me punishment enough."

"So Henry sailed, did he," I said thoughtfully. "It seems reasonable to assume that news of the troubles at the Tower has spread about." Richard nodded and looked around to make sure no one was about. He continued: "Buckingham knew; he told me so, thinking he could use it as a bargaining chip. But I had him isolated from the other prisioners at once and had Sir James Tyrell guard him." I sniggered:

"Well, they could jaw about it all day but, believe you me, I bet they didn't."

"Exactly so. Anyhow, there wasn't time since I hurried Buckingham's execution along," confirmed Richard.

"No last words from the scaffold?" I asked.

"D'you know, I think Sir James talked him out of it." We were both quiet for a bit, one didn't really know whether to laugh or cry. Then Richard said:

"Oh, and by the way, while we are on that subject, I learnt from my spies in Paris that during a meeting of the French council of state, some one suggested that the 'English solution' be considered for dealing with their own underage monarch problem." I giggled:

"Hey, Richard, you may have started a trend! The wicked uncle. In fact, the wicked …. And choose which ever family member you like. Mother, sister, aunt, cousin and so on." But Richard wasn't amused.

"Such a bloody waste of time," he shouted, banging his tumbler down on the table, spilling wine all over the place, resulting in a new jug of wine having to be brought in. After things had settled down, he continued: "I don't like wasting my time on all this foolery when there are matters of greater importance to be dealt with.

"Why, London is a cesspool and we need to improve our roads but, Lord, I never have time to turn my attention to doing something about it. All these political matters come up and one must deal with them. And if I pass on the responsibility to one of my so-called councilors, he will think I've just given him a free pass to steal and plunder the commons. I'd give up the throne, I would, but to whom? Would you like to be king for a while, Gaius?" I shuddered.

"Perish the thought!"

The only other notable happening at this time was that the Princess Elisabeth of York, Ma Wydville's older daughter, turned up, hat in hand and carrying a small bag. We were all in the drawing rom when she turned up and not one of use was not non-plused. Anne was the one to react first. She jumped up and stretched her arms towards Elisabeth who fell into them. Well, I could iagine her home hadn't been happy or carefree.

"My dear," cooed Anne, stroking her hair. "You are most welcome here, most welcome." Elisabeth sniffed.

"Mother said I might come," she answered and a few tears fell. "She said I needed to learn about court life." Richard and I exchanged glances. Not much to learn in this mournful place.

I'd seen her before, of course. A waif of a thing, at least that was my first impression. But she was tall, like her parents, and had the family's blue eyes and blond hair. Put some colour in her face, feed her for a while and stiffen her spine and she wouldn't be bad at all. Anne continued:

"That's wonderful, my dear. You will be such a comfort to me. Come, I will show to your room." And the two felt, leaving Richard and me alone. We exchanged glances. Richard was the first to speak.

"What's she doing here, Gaius? A spy within the walls?" I shook my nogging.

"Maybe but I hardly think so. If what we think is true – and don't interrupt me, Richard, I just can't discuss the matter anymore. I think you should just accept her and try to leave her at ease. If I know anything about Ma Wydville, she probably just wanted some more space and throwing Elisabeth out was one body less, no pun intended.

So the discussion about Elisabeth ceased and she stayed with up creeping about and hanging close to Anne.

"She's never had a decent mother," whispered Anne. "When you consider how busy Ma Wydville always was." Yeah, thinks I, all that plotting tends to take up once time.

Elisabeth only went to visit her mother if pushed by Anne so the spy within the walls seemed theory was dropped.

14

Richard's Agenda

Come January and all was peace and quiet in Richard's working chamber. Richard was at a desk overflowing with paperwork, ledgers and stuff, while secretaries and scribes hurried here and there, some taking signed papers out, some bringing papers to be signed in. All wore felt shoes as Richard had forbidden any shuffling or scraping of leather boots in his office. He said scuffling feet distracted him.

He had tried to do something about the scratching of quills but that would have to wait about 600 years until the biro arrived in the 20th century. I, as usual, had settled down in a window embrasure, observing the comings and goings between naps. All this showed Richard in is old light – he was definitely a workaholic and his staff was being worn to a frazzle.

So there we were, all peaceful and quiet and I thought to myself: this is what a king should be – busy with his duties to the kingdom. Richard would have made a good CEO. But then there was a deal of shouting in the anteroom, the door was flung upon and the Duke of Northumberland stormed in. Richard looked up, put down his pen, leaned back in his chair and steepled his fingers.

"My dear Percy," he said quietly, "is this how you enter your sovereign's private office, just barge in as if it were a public house? Would you have done that if my brother were still king?" Henry Percy didn't bother to answer but threw himself into a nearby chair.

"Tell me," he snarled, "that it isn't true!"

"I might," answered Richard, "if I knew what it was."

"About Parliament!" Richard raised his eyebrows as high as they could go.

"What about it?"

"There are rumours that you have called a Parliament!"

"And so I have. The Commons will meet on 23 January." Percy got up and started walking about in a rage.

"What for? What do that lot of shopkeepers and busybodies have to do with the running this kingdom? It is our affair; we, the nobility, lay down the law."

"That," replied Richard nastily, "is because you do not know the law. Parliament writes the laws and the king approves and signs them and it is his responsibility to see they are upheld. My dear Percy, that is what is called checks and balances or, if you prefer, advise and consent. So neither king or commons have too much power and neither can be tempted to abuse it. I confess that my dear brother Edward did not see it that way. Anyhow, Parliament will meet on the 23rd and the first item on the agenda will be to confirm me as king, through a private statute, *Titulus Regius.*" Percy stopped and stared at him.

"Oh," he said, "and you think that this piece of paper will keep you safe on the throne?" Richard took up his pen and rolled it between his fingers.

"No," he said, "because the nobility will sooner or later challenge me, no matter how many acts of Parliament there may be confirming me as king. The nobility, unfortunately, do not respect or uphold the laws of the realm. So, yes, when Tudor gets his act together – if ever – he will not care, no, not one wit – whether Parliament has confirmed me or not. For him, and all those who want to be king, Parliament is merely academic." Percy got up, but sat down again.

"Tell me, Richard, will you use this partliament to give me back the lands that were stolen from me by your deceased brother – Edward, of course – but that nonetheless are Percy property?" Richard thought for a moment. Then he said:

"Nooo, my friend, for that is not the purpose of Parliament. But if you will take your case to court, I will see to it you get a favorable hearing." Percy threw up his hands and walked out. Just to keep the record straight, Percy did get his lands back- eventually.

"He didn't call you 'my dread lord'", I said, "I just thought I'd mention it, you know."

"Gaius, all those guys, Percy, Buckingham et al, behave as if they own me because they think they put me where I am. Ergo, the lack of respect. Also, they know that I am unwilling to throw people into the Tower or hack heads off on their say-so." A frisson ran through him. "Yes, it is a perilous path but nevertheless, I shall do what I think is right, come what may. This country," he continued, looking up at the ornate ceiling, "is frankly a mess. Hardly surprising seeing that we, who should be its guardians and protectors, have spent the last I don't know how long hacking each other to pieces." Well, that was yesterday's news and I wasn't about to get into ancient history.

Richard continued: "Just before we were so rudely interruped by that stupid rebellion, I had a few thoughts on how this country can be improved so that it serves its citizens and not just special interest groups. Would you like to hear about it?" Well, not really, but I agreed because I knew I would have to anyway.

Richard droned on for a time; when his voice became lower, I napped but each time he came to a point with special emphasis, he raised his voice and banged on tables or chests or bookcases or whatever and I awoke with a start. When it was all over, he asked: "Well, Gaius, what do you think?" I said:

"Brilliant, Richard, just brilliant. Go for it." He stroked his chin and had a smug and self-satisfied look on his face. "But there's just one bit you could add." I told him and his face lit up.

15

Richard's Parliament

January would not have been my choice for a meeting of the
House of Commons. May or June at the earliest or preferably July.
But, for reasons known only to Richard himself, January it was,
despite the weather – snow and ice in abundance, freezing cold and
a nasty cutting wind. I asked him why he didn't wait until at least
April but he just said:

"I haven't much time." I didn't ask any more questions. In fact,
what did I care – until he suggested I go with him; here I took a firm
stand: not a hope. It made him quite cross.

"All you do is sleep," he objected, "and you might as well sleep in
Parliament as anywhere else." But I was adamant – and so I stayed at
the palace, in the main drawing room where there was a nice fire. I
stretched out on the mantelpiece, curled up and went to sleep.

A ruckus in the hall woke me up. The party was back. Richard had
dragged poor Anne with him and I saw them shedding off their work
clothes – ermine capes and crowns and such – handing the lot to
underlings. Anne looked done in, waved at me, then came into the
room. I got in first.

"Anne!" I exclaimed in my best party voice. "You look great!
That blue satin really does it for you." She sneered at me:

"I couldn't wear my red velvet today! My maid is still trying to
brush the cat hairs off! I was most upset." I purred.

"Wonderful stuff, velvet. So sleek and soft. I had a beautiful nap."
Richard coughed:

"I suppose," he said to Anne, careful as any husband about to contradict his wife, "you'd left it lying on your bed." Anne turned to him, and she wasn't pleased. She snapped:

"How did you guess?" This was the only time I'd seen Anne out of temper. Then she shrugged her shoulders and turned her back on us. "Oh, the two of you are hopeless. I'm off to rest. All this has put me out of temper." She turned to Richard: "No more parliaments, you hear me? At least, not if I have to go!" She disappeared, followed by her ladies who hoped her bad temper wouldn't spill over on them.

Richard sat down in his favorite chair close to the fire, muttering:

"I can't see why she's tired; she slept through most of it." To me: "I could have done without the fuss about the velvet dress," he snarled. I stretched and yawned.

"Sorry, pal," I said, not at all sorry, "but a cat has to do what a cat has to do. Velvet is especially appealing to cats." He turned his back on me in a huff and addressed Sir William Catesby who had come, so to speak, in his wake. "Take a load off, Sir William, put your feet up." Sir William plumped himself down in a well-cushioned chair with a sigh of relief, his feet on a footstool.

"Glad that's over," he said, stretching out.

"Sir William," Richard informed me, "is now Speaker of the House of Commons and a damned good one, too! Why, we had the lot eating out of our hands, didn't we, Sir William?" Sir William sighed again and answered with closed eyes:

"If you say so, my Lord, if you say so." Richard shouted for menials and strong drink. "Better set up sort of a bar over there," he told the butler, waving to a corner of the room. "We may have callers. And bring some snacks, anything you can dig up that doesn't have mold on it or tries to run away." The menials snapped to it and in a thrice it was all there – Richard's and Sir William's wine, bits of cheese and meat and bread and so forth. For me, water and my favorite tuna snaquettes. They knew my ways.

"Ahh," sighed Richard in his turn, stretching his legs and taking a deep draught. I swished my tail about. I said:

"Come on, Richard, let's have all the dirt."

"As you may know," started Richard looking into the middle distance, "the first day of a House of Commons session is attended by both Lords and Commons, though, of course, the Lords have no say in House deliberations." Oh, vow, that must have given them a real incentive to turn up. On the other hand, it could be dangerous to stay away; they needed to keep a finger on Richard's pulse. "We had a full house, didn't we, Sir William?" he continued. Sir William grunted his agreement. Richard continued dreamily: "Lords on the right, Commons on the left." He took another swig and continued staring into the middle distance. Sir William was fast asleep. I got impatient.

"Come on, what happened? Who was there?" Richard came out of his reverie with a start.

"Right! On the Lords' side, all the usual suspects, Northumberland, Norfolk, Stanley and so on. Our friend Buckingham, I am sure, was sorely missed. Of the Commons, you wouldn't know any of their names but Sir William called the roll and every member was there." Sir William opened his eyes, waved his empty mug and looked around.

"Ahh, thank you, my lad," he said graciously to the menial who rushed to top him up. He swilled some down and then decided he needed to add to the conversation: "The king – that's you, my Lord - opened the session; quite unheard of, you know." Yes, I understood that the king usually sat in the gallery making notes of all the things he didn't like and would veto. And all those he would execute for being uppity. Sir William woke up properly and continued: "Especially unusual was that King Richard said he wished to place before the House the government's plan of action for the next twelve months." Sir William sniggered: "Usually, the king only goes to the Commons when he's run out of cash."

"The first thing on the agenda," continued Richard, his eyes closed, hands clasped around his glass, "was the *Titulus Regius*." Indeed. I swished my tail. By this Act the progeny of both his brothers Edward and George were excluded from the succession, which went to Richard and his progeny. Richard squirmed a bit. I wasn't surprised. He glanced my way. "I know you don't approve but I had to have it!" Sure. Dot your i's and cross your t's. What's done is done. He went on: "The Speaker read the Act and the Commons voted on it." Richard chewed thoughtfully on a sausage and took a sip of wine. "I was very clear in my instructions. I stressed that, if they wished, they could retire to discuss the matter; I also gave them the option of voting by secret ballot." Sir William surfaced once more:

"They decided on an open vote; I called the roll and the Act was unanimously approved." I looked up at the ceiling: why was I not surprised? Taking my eyes back to Richard, I said:

"What would you have done, Richard, if the vote had gone against you?" Richard scratched his cheek and wrinkled his nose:

"You know, I only thought of it when Sir William was counting the yeas and nays; I don't know, really, I might just have dumped all the panoply of kingship and walked out." Now, that would have been something to see. On the other hand, there wasn't really any option. It was either Richard or the last remaining kid, Edward, and I don't think that one was high on anyone's list. Richard cracked his knuckles – a nasty sound – and went on.

"Then we discussed benevolences, arbitrary taxes created by my late brother, imposed as he saw fit and never accounted for." Richard rubbed his hand together. "When I announced that these were to be repelled, there were excited whispers and smiles among the commons – some cheered – but sour looks from the nobility." I yawned:

"No prizes," was my comment, "for guessing who paid and who benefited." Richard ignored me. He continued, Sir William snoring peacefully next to him. "After that, the commons became friskier and more interested in the proceedings."

Noises in the hall told us new arrivals were being shown in. The first was Sir James Tyrrell. Richard welcomed him with open arms:

"Sir James! You've become quite a stranger. You must call more often. Name your poison." Sir James thought he'd have a gin and tonic; a menial hurried to get it. Then came the Duke of Northumberland with the Dukes of Sussex and Norfolk. And Lord Stanley. It says a lot about Lord Stanley that he dropped in for Happy Hour with his stepson's main rival. But then, a free drink is not to be sneezed at.

Other guests arrived, churchmen, aldermen, members of the professional guilds, in other words, rich commoners or, in modern parlance, the bourgeoisie. Now, Stalin,[8] not of fond memory, thought the bourgeoisie appeared at the time of the French revolution. An ignoramus. These gentlemen have been with us since the days of Rome, known then as the equites, when aristocrats weren't supposed to be 'in trade'. As the man said: 'the bourgeoisie will always be with us.' Amazing how popular the concept of not making money while having it has always been and continues to be popular. There is something in it, though. Think. The bourgeoisie make the money while the aristocrats are sent out to glorious deaths on myriads of battlefields.

Some of the newcomers took up chairs near Richard so we became quite a cozy little group. Once the crowd had been served – whiskeys and sodas and whatever – Richard rose, held up his glass and said:

"Glad you could all come. I was just giving Gaius the rundown of what went on today in the Commons!" No one looked surprised; by that time they were used to me. Richard continued: "So now you're here you can all contribute with your opinions." He snapped his fingers and a menial came hurrying up. "Call my secretary. I want him to take notes." The guests looked slightly discomfited. Richard smiled: "The work for the realm never stops." A young clerk came scuttling in with quill and paper and unobtrusively took a seat in a corner. Norfolk was the first to speak. He cleared his throat noisily:

"I thought it was noble of you to confirm all grants and estates of land made to Lady Elizabeth Grey, despite the invalidity of her marriage to your late brother, king Edward IV." Richard looked modest and steepled his fingers:

"It is my firm policy to favor my enemies. It makes them look ungrateful and churlish. And I am quite sure Elizabeth is not about to refuse." Norfolk chuckled.

"Just don't expect her to walk through that door anytime soon to thank you," he said wryly. I quoted, looking straight at Lord Stanley: *"Ingratitude, more strong than traitor's arms[9]. Arms,* in this case," I explained to the company still eyeballing Lord Stanley, "meaning

---

8   Dictator, USSR, 20th century
9   *Julius Caesar* Wm Shakespeare

weapons rather than *upper limbs*." Lord Stanley stood up, looking flustered:

"My Lord," he said, "I was going to thank you for turning over my wife's estates to me. I can assure you that both I and Lady Margaret are most grateful." Richard peered at him:

"I must admit that motherhood seems to excuse a multitude of sins. I do not expect your wife, Lord Stanley, to abandon her son and I shall not penalize her for sticking with him." Lord Stanley bowed and sat down, looking relieved. After that little aside, Richard continued: "I hope you will all agree that protection of property rights is fundamental to the good order of society." Dubious looks all around, except from Sir William who was still asleep. "We all know what went on during our lawless years, that is, the civil war; the same property sold again and again, and at the end most unlawfully appropriated. The endless lawsuits tied up our legal system for years to the detriment of other, more important, cases. You, Northumberland, as well as our dear departed Buckingham, were both victims of land grabs for the greater glory of the Wydvilles." He held out his arm and a menial dashed up with the wine jug.

"Indeed," Northumberland nodded his head sagely. Richard continued:

"So my proposal against fraudulent sales of land is sound and will benefit everyone." The company nodded, hoping their ill-gotten gains would not be flushed out. Sir William stirred as if his name had been called:

"From this point on, all sales and/or gifts of land will favor the buyer; any burden to be held against the seller and his heirs." No one looked particularly pleased. Richard did not seem to notice but continued:

"Property transfers will be made in the Court of Common Pleas and notices thereof sent to the appropriate county officials." He looked downright pleased with himself. Well, nobody jumped for joy but there were vague murmurs of approval. Norfolk, Richard's staunchest supporter, then said, touching on a less controversial topic:

"I think the subject of bail was equally important and that a person be considered innocent until proven guilty. It will protect anyone from imprisonment before trial, and forfeiture of their property before conviction." Richard looked pleased:

"I knew you would like that one, Norfolk," he said. "I am calling it the Clarence Act in honor of my late brother George." More murmurs of approval. Norfolk went on:

"But I'm not sure I understand revising juror qualifications." Richard slapped his thigh and sat up:

"I want to put an end to juror corruption. If jurors must own substantial property, they will be less easy to bribe. I think I've been reasonable: 20 shillings worth of freehold land or 26 shillings, eight pence of copyhold land." No one looked too put out; on the other hand no one shouted their approval. They had sufficient cash to bribe even those above the property limits set by Richard. Oblivious of this, he called for more refreshments and additional snacks and saw to it that everyone was comfortable. After a deep swallow from his refilled mug, Norfolk murmured:

"Well, Richard, you seem determined to have law and order in our courts. Not a bad thing, I guess." I turned over on my stomach and murmured:

"I'm sure the nobility likes the old ways best – management by chaos. Something happens and you react. Laws? Of course: for peasants and common folk. However, if thieves and murderers were prosecuted with no regard to social status, there wouldn't be many of the nobility left." Richard frowned and the others looked daggers at me. Northumberland bridged the awkward silence:

"You also brought up quite a few items on commercial matters." Richard nodded his head vigorously:

"Commerce is the backbone of our nation. I want common standards for cloth, the proper measurement of wine and oil, and strict rules on imports and exports to protect local manufacturers. Imports will be taxed reasonably. However, I will have no duties on printing presses and books. Everyone should be able to read and have access to books and such." Someone murmured under his breath (but I heard him).

"That's just what England needs. Literate peasants!" Then Richard expounded on the price controls to protect local industry. I shut my eyes. Price controls! Every demagogue's favorite gambit.

I'm sure the Neolithic and Egyptians had price controls. Rome was famous for fixing the price of grain – bread and circuses, you know; politicians down the ages have used controls to keep the head count – or the mob – quiet. It will never go out of style. But I kept my peace.

So it went on and only the unlimited supply of drinks and snacks kept the audience in place. When Richard said:

"I am also insisting that the clergy collect their tithes. No more farming it out to tax collectors!" I looked around at the clergy present. No happy faces. Squeezing the populace for the dismes would not make for popular prelates among the hoi polloi. The next two points, a College of Arms to deal with hereditary and genealogy, did not get a lot of applause, either; this could complicate the lives of the upper classes. This was followed by a Court of Requests to ensure the common people access to the legal system which must have cooked Richard's goose as far as the upper classes were concerned. All worthy causes but none would endear Richard to his peers. Shades of impeachment? At that point, I fell asleep and so missed the next bits. I woke up when Richard started on taxes:

"My friends," he was now pacing backwards and forwards. "The first and fundamental duty of a king is to see that each citizen – commons, clergy and nobility – pay only those taxes approved by the House of Commons. The king must run his household on the stipend set aside for this purpose; wars, except in defense of the realm, must all be sanctioned by the Commons." Northumberland coughed and asked:

"So, my Lord, you're not planning any wars? That seems odd, especially from a king who, so to speak, was born into one." Richard pointed a finger at him and said, narrowing his eyes to mere slits.

"Exactly! And that's why I'm determined there will be no more. It's a waste of men and materials and when it's all over no one remembers what it was all about. As for 'glory and honor', that's for the birds." He looked at Northumberland's crestfallen face. "But you, my dear Percy, will see plenty of action in your patch. The Scots will always be at it." Northumberland cheered up a bit. Richard continued:

"Each of you must keep your home counties safe and your people under control. I'm sure you'll not lack for activity." No, what they would lack would be war profiteering, ransoms from important prisoners – and here I'm sure Percy knew he would have trouble getting any even if he captured the king of Scots, the Scots being known for their miserliness. Richard was blissfully unaware of the glum atmosphere and went back to taxes: "If my government needs extra cash, it shall borrow in the normal manner, pay interest on the principle and safeguard repayment." Northumberland and Suffolk exchanged looks. An honest king. What an anomaly. Norfolk then spoke up:

"What about this constitution you spoke of? I'm not sure I quite got that." Richard was more than happy to explain.

"A Constitution for the realm to be binding on all Englishmen. Here is how I see its first paragraph:

> *"We the People, in order to establish justice,*
> *insure domestic tranquility, provide for the*
> *common defence, promote the general welfare,*
> *and secure the blessings of liberty to ourselves and*
> *our posterity, do ordain and establish this Constitution*
> *for the British Isles.*

"You must be mad," protested Northumberland quite forgetting himself, "you're lumping all Englishmen together as if there was no difference in degree. Surely you cannot expect everyone to be treated alike – after all, the aristocracy must come first, then the clergy and then..." he trailed off as I intoned:

> *throw away respect,*
> *Tradition, form and ceremonious duty,*
> *For you have but mistook me [Richard II] all this while:*
> *I live with bread like you, feel want,*
> *Taste grief, need friends: subjected thus,*
> *How can you say to me, I am a king?"[10]*

---

[10]   *Richard II* Wm Shakespeare.

Silence. And looks at me. I said:

"It means, gentlemen, all men have equal needs. Let's not run away with the idea that all men are born equal but some are more equal than others." This sort of broke up the evening. As Suffolk was leaving, I heard him say:

"Richard, I really would get rid of that cat."

When we were alone again, Richard rubbed his hands:

"Well," he said grinning, "that sure stirred things up although I'm afraid they didn't quite get the last part." I was having a nice long stretch.

"No doubt but they got the gist of it," I answered. "But I'm afraid you haven't won any popularity points from your nearest and dearest. As far as I can see, English kings have always preferred management by chaos and the nobility is all for it. Easy pickings, you might say." Richard ignored me.

"The purpose of kingship should be to make sure the laws are fair and obeyed to the letter. That's how you get a just society." I murmured:

"Don't break an arm." Richard frowned:

"What do you mean, why should I break an arm?"

"Trying to pat yourself on the back!"

As Richard snored away, I became pensive. Had Richard been a modern prime minister, he would sure have gotten the common vote out for his party. However, if his objective was to cozy up to those who were responsible for bringing him to power – all those Dukes and Earls and such – he was way off base and it might all come back to bite him. Impeachment was in the air.

16
Interlude in Paris

Mother and son were enjoying a quiet happy hour together although the atmosphere was sombre. Lady Margaret sipped at her white wine. Henry was making short work of a whisky and soda. Henry said, looking into the distance:

"Perhaps I should give this whole thing up and look for a job." His mother glared at him.

"My dear," she said acidly, "it seems to me you are looking for a job." He glanced at her sideways:

"I hate to tell you this, mother, but my last interview went really badly." She sniffed:

"Hardly your fault; but I must say there should be a better way of predicting the weather than just staring at the sky." Henry stretched out:

"Red sunset at night, sailor's delight, red sun in the morning, sailor take warning." Lady Margaret did not seem amused.

"Very pretty, I am sure, but hardly scientific." Her son answered:

"There should be a better way of building ships. Mine were blown all over the channel. It's a miracle any of those onboard survived." Silence for a bit while drinks were swallowed meditatively. Then mother said:

"Lucky the winds blew you so-called fleet towards France and not England." Food for thought. Then Henry changed the subject:

"But, seriously, mother, do you think I still have a chance? Richard seems to be settling down quite nicely. Pity we can't use the princes' fate to stir up the populace against him. That would go down a real treat with the great unwashed."

"It would be a terrible idea," answered Lady Margaret firmly. "Don't even think of it. We don't know who actually did the deed but I'm sure Richard does. And if the real story came out, we'd be finished, Tudors and Wydvilles. Remember always there is a witness who can cook all our geese." Henry held up his hands, shaking his head:

"I would imagine myself that whoever done it, so to speak, is long gone from this world. At least, that's what I would have done." Lady Margaret shook her head as if in despair.

"You can be sure Richard has that guy alive and kicking. It's his surety for our silence as was keeping those boys in the Tower. Dead men tell no tales but it works the other way, too." Henry sighed:

"I was just joking. But, you know, if we come through, we will have to face this problem sooner or later." His mother looked at him frowning:

"What task, what are you talking about?" Henry got up and waved his arms around.

"Think, mother, think! Some day someone will have to explain what happened to those boys. It's not just something that will go away. Richard has done quite well keeping a lid on it and, of course, if I become king, which would mean Richard is dead, I would blame it all on him." Lady Margaret snorted:

"I'm surprised it hasn't come out already," she said, "seems to me lots of people know – we do, all the Wydvilles, Buckingham knew and I take it you told the Regent Anne to get her to help you." This was a thorny point since whatever investment Regent Anne had made had gone down the drain.

"Nooo," said Henry slowly, "in fact, I didn't. I told her I was going to rescue the true king and put him on the throne." Lady Margaret snorted again.

"What a hypocrite. Regent Anne is very far from being stupid. She must be, to keep her position. You need to give her more credit for brains, Henry, or you'll come a cropper. She will have to finance you again. But I think she knows anyway and so do other high officials in France." Henry rubbed his chin thoughtfully.

"You're right, Mother, truth is always the best. It's so difficult to keep lies straight in your head. So from now on I shall tell the truth and shame the devil."

17

When Sorrows Come

Holidays are very nice but there are times when I would just like to be off somewhere else as fast as I ever can. And this was one of those moments. Edward, Richard's only son, was ill. He was lying on his unhygienic matress with all those unhygienic pillows and sheets and what have you. How I would have liked to wisk him off to the Cedars and Lebanon hospital in Sao Paulo! Because I was lying on his blanket and I knew that no one around here was going to figure out what was wrong with him and it might be catching. Richard and Anne sat on either side of the bed, trying to look brave and not to cry. They knew what was coming.

Anne said through restrained sobs:

"It's true, isn't it, Gaius, that a cat can take away dark vibes?" Well, I suppose I knew what she meant and it was all poppycock. But what can one do? So I cleared my throat and said, trying not to sound as if I were lying:

"I'm doing my best, Anne!" A whole load of apothecaries, surgeons, doctors (I don't know what they called them then) were standing along the walls looking disgruntled. One said:

"Leeches, your grace. Leeches to extract the poisons. I beg you to allow me apply half-a-dozen to his grace." Richard looked at me. I shook my head and whispered:

"Don't think of it. Don't make the kid's last moments a misery." Another specimen added:

"I have a poultice here, my Lord, guaranteed to draw the poison. I beg you, my Lord." Anne started to go into convolutions of sobbing and Richard motioned for a lady in waiting to remove her from the bedside to an armchair further back in the room. Richard looked at me:

"What harm can there be in trying out one of these remedies? And I don't know why I am listening to you? You're just a cat." I snarled at him.

"A cat I may be but I know a charlatan when I see one. Those guys, they don't know anything, but anything about the human body." Richard's eyes flashed.

"And I suppose you know! What is the matter with Edward?"

"I'm not quite sure but I think he has a ruptured appendix."

"And what can we do for it?"

"Cut it out!" Richard blanched.

"You mean, cut the boy open to take whatever this it is out?" I sighed.

"Sorry, Richard, I know it can't be done. If you did manage it, he would die of an infection. The hygiene around here is appalling." At that moment, Edward opened his eyes and gripped my paw.

"Gaius," he whispered, "how did that poem go, the one about falling asleep?" I cleared my throat. This was too much and for a moment I couldn't get my mouth open; then I managed:

> *"We are such stuff*
> *as dreams are made of*
> *and our little life is rounded*
> *with a sleep."[11]*

Edward smiled. His grip on my paw slackened. He was gone. I thought Anne would sob her heart out. In fact, I thought they both would.

> *When sorrows come, they come not single spies but in*
> *battalions. [12]*

This time it was Queen Anne. I was in the window embrasure, Richard was sitting by her bed holding her hand and a fistful of ladies were milling about – albeit quietly – wringing their hands and

---

[11]   *A Summer Night's Dream* Wm Shakespeare.
[12]   *Hamlet* Wm Shakespeare.

good for nothing. The usual suspects who believed – or pretend to believe they are apothecaries, surgeons or whatnot, were hanging about. Richard wouldn't let me anywhere near Anne. Her breathing was labored and she was so thin and weak you could have knocked her over with a wildflower – if you could have gotten her to stand.

On the other side of her bed was her niece, Elizabeth, in floods of tears. Really, if I didn't know that the Wydvilles loathed Richard I would never have guessed by looking at this Elisabeth. Then, Elizabeth Wydville seemed to trust Richard with whatever kids of hers needed a change.

I had no idea what was wrong with Anne. I mean, she wasn't swollen anywhere which ruled out most cancers. It might of course have been leukemia or malnutrition – I mean, the way these people eat would kill a hippopotamus.

Suddenly, I felt myself wrenched from my embrasure and floating in mid-air. Elisabeth had grabbed me and put me down on Anne's bed.

"Cats are supposed to heal," she said to me, "so get on with it." Anne smiled tiredly at me.

"Sorry, Gaius," she said in her low voice, "I know we've had our differences – about dresses and cloaks and so on – but I do love you and I will miss you, despite my sables." I coughed in embarrassment. Edward, her late son, and I had once had a snuggle in her sable coat. When she found us, we were not popular.

"Anne," I answered, "I swear that if I could do anything for you, I would. The best I can say is that our relationship might have resulted in us both being burnt as witch and succubus." Anne shivered.

"Yes, being a cat can have its drawbacks." She held out her hand to me and I put my paw in it. "Don't you have a poem for me?" she asked. I sighed. A long association with poets has its consequences. I cleared my throat and looked at the ceiling.

> *"She walks in beauty, like the night*
> *Of cloudless climes and starry skies;*
> *And all that's best of dark and bright*
> *Meet in her aspect and her eyes;*
> *Thus mellowed to that tender light*
> *Which heaven to gaudy day denies.*

> *"One shade the more, one ray the less,*
> *Had half impaired the nameless grace*
> *Which waves in every raven tress,*
> *Or softly lightens o'er her face;*
> *Where thoughts serenely sweet express,*
> *How pure, how dear their dwelling-place.*
>
> *"And on that cheek, and o'er that brow,*
> *So soft, so calm, yet eloquent,*
> *The smiles that win, the tints that glow,*
> *But tell of days in goodness spent,*
> *A mind at peace with all below,*
> *A heart whose love is innocent!"*[13]

Richard laid his face on the bed and sobbed. Anne said:

"Gaius, how is it you always know the right thing to say?" She looked at Elizabeth. "Wasn't that a lovely poem, my dear niece?" Then Elizabeth started crying. Anne and I looked at each other. My thoughts said: 'I'm glad, dearest Anne, you will be spared the last chapter of this gruesome story. You and your son both.' Anne gave me a knowing look as if she understood. Then she sank back on to her pillows and left us.

---

[13]   George Gordon, Lord Byron.

18

A Proposal

We were in a salon; it was way past Happy Hour but Richard didn't seem to have enough energy either to have a drink, his supper or go to bed. He just sat, rocking side to side, his face buried in his hand.

"Gaius, I so miss my Anne and my Edward, I want to feel sorry for myself but I can't, not after all that's happened." Richard was inconsolable but with the sanitary conditions being what they were and zero medical knowledge, what could one expect? I sighed and said:

"*When sorrows come, they come not as single spies but in battalions.*"[14] Richard looked up:

"That's pretty good, Gaius, and exactly how I feel though I would never have been able to express it so well." No, Richard. I love you but a Will you are not.

Richard had a drink then and another and went on with his catalogue of woes.

"It seems that our friend Henry Tudor is on the march. His patron, the regent Anne, has put ships and troops at his command so we shall have him here anon." I lay my head on my front paws.

"Well, at least we know for sure why the kids were murdered. Or is it just a coincidence that once they were no more Henry got off his backside and went into action?"

Richard shook his head. 'Nough said, end of story. I continued:

---

[14] *Hamlet* Wm Shakespeare.

"I take it a lot of the nobility will go for him. I don't really understand why, after all he's a nobody and his claim to the throne is so tenuous it might be said to be non-existent. But your pals are going to welcome him with open arms – and make him king. And, I ask myself, why should they? They are giving power of life and death over the whole population of England together with all its riches, to what amounts to be a total stranger. There's got to be something wrong somewhere." I sighed in my turn.

"This king business really floors me. Cats would never do that, give away their power. Why do people need kings who more often than not become tyrants? Present company excepted."

"Well, Gaius," answered Richard, "I cannot give you a sensible answer. Having been king myself, I have experienced what it is to have absolute power at my disposal. I did not use it but I am sure Henry will. And, as you say, his claim has so many ups and downs it might be a game of snakes and ladders and it may be the only way for him to stay afloat."

"You forget, my dear Richard, that there are no more Lancasters left. He is the last one. The only game in town." Richard looked gloomy:

"Everyone seems to have forgotten the other Edward, Clarence's son. I have a feeling, Gaius, his future does not look bright and shiny." We thought about it. In fact, Henry VII would keep that Edward locked up in the Tower until Ferdinand and Isabella of Spain demanded he be put to death before they would send their daughter, Catalina, to England to marry Henry's son Arthur. Catalina, or Katherine of Aragon, had a rotten life. Perhaps that was payback. To round things out, Margaret, Clarence's daughter, lived to be an old lady, before Henry VIII decided to chop off her head. Charming lot, the Tudors.

There came a timid knock on the door. For all Richard's talk against abuse of power, he'd become so frustrated at having found that a king was mostly expected to sign papers that got people's heads chopped off, making him feared far and wide. He growled:

"What is it? Go away!" But the door opened nonetheless and a little white face peeped around it.

"Well," cried Richard almost savagely, "so come in or stay out but make up your mind!"

"Richard," I whispered, "put on your party manners for a minute. I think it's a girl and if it is, it's probably one Elizabeth." Richard sighed, got up and opened the door fully.

"Elizabeth!" he gasped in surprise. "What do you want this time of night?"

"Can I come in, uncle?"

"Well, shouldn't you have a lady in waiting with you or some sort of female companion as chaperone? Does your mother know you are here?" Elizabeth shook her head and came inRichard closed the door behind her. She said:

"No, my mother doesn't know I am here. At least, not right here" Then she saw me. "Can't the cat be the chaperone?" I looked at Richard and Richard looked at me.

"Suppose so although it's rather unorthodox," he said as he got her a chair and sat down himself. "You were a good little maid for my poor Anne in her last days," he continued softly, "and I shall always remember that." A snivel from Elizabeth.

"I was very fond of Aunt Anne. I'm sorry she's dead, and poor Edward too." For a moment I thought she meant her brother but then it dawned on me that it must be her cousin, Richard's son. No one had mentioned her brothers for ages although a bulletin about their well-being was issued at regular intervals by Sir Brakenbury, the Lieutenant of the Tower. Elizabeth said:

"My mother wants me to marry Henry Tudor." I pricked up my ears. Now, this was very interesting. "But I don't want to marry a man I've never seen. And people don't say nice things about him. It seems he's mean; in money matters, that is. And I find that a disagreeable trait, don't you?" This subject was so delicate that neither Richard nor I knew how to handle it. If Elisabeth the Queen was reaching out to Henry Tudor, it could only mean... But Elisabeth interrupted my thought process by saying: "Mother thinks that if I marry the Lancastrian heir, as I am the Yorkist heir, we can put this whole thing behind us."

Well, that begged the question that neither Richard nor I wanted ask. Instead, Richard said slowly:

"That would mean that Henry Tudor is ready to invade England. How nice. We can go back to our wars which will keep us all busy and out of the public houses." Elisabeth looked somewhat bemused but continued:

"Oh, Uncle, I don't want any more wars. I've had a better idea, an idea that will make it possible for all parties to be reconciled immediately." Richard leaned forward and asked gently:

"And what idea is that, Elizabeth?"

"Why," she said as calmly as you like, "I should marry you instead." We were both speechless. Impediments and obstacles to such a step whirled around the room and I knew that Richard could sense them too. All sorts of questions would be asked that I am sure no one, on either side, would like raked up. However, when Richard applied himself to answer her, he said gently:

"Elizabeth, I couldn't possibly marry you. You're my darling niece, my dear brother's daughter. To me, you will always be a child." Elizabeth shook her head.

"Lots of kings and princes and Dukes marry their nieces, cousins, sisters-in-laws; they'd even marry their sisters if it were in their interest and the Pope could be squared away. It's not so uncommon." That might be so, but I'll be damned if I could think of an example, except for some Portuguese princess who did marry an uncle in the 18th century. Salome, too, married an uncle. Richard shook his head.

"My darling niece, it just won't do. I can appreciate how, in your mind, it would solve all the dynastic problems but my conscience would not allow it. So let's hear no more about it and let each of us go to our fates as God wills." She threw himself in his arms and had a good cry. Then she said:

"Don't, uncle, don't let this happen to me." Richard caressed her head and took out a handkerchief and dried her eyes.

"Well, you know, Elizabeth, it may happen that Henry Tudor will be lost at sea or that he will be killed in battle or that I will win. So don't give up hope just yet." He got her to her feet and took her back to her quarters.

After Richard returned, he got himself another mug of wine while I sat on my window embrasure and switched my tail. For a while, we were silent. Then I said:

"When we said the Wydvilles benefited from the murder of the boys, we must take that with a grain of salt." Richard looked at me irritated:

"We have discussed this to death, Gaius, and I thought we were agreed that the Wydvilles were the guilty party. Are you now changing your mind? Not," he continued nastily, "that it would make any difference." My tail whipped backwards and forwards, a sure sign of irritation in a cat.

"No, Richard, I haven't, as you so picturesquely call it, changed my mind. We are agreed that the Wydvilles are responsible but the Wydvilles aren't the answer to the question *who benefits?"*

"For God's sake, Gaius, do you think someone would murder their own kids if there was no benefit in it for them? We agreed they did it for power."

"True," I conceded, "but they didn't look far enough. Their bid for power ended with the boys' deaths. So, you could say that in the short term they benefitted as it opened the possibility of taking up arms against you, getting you off the throne... and here is the rub: because they had no candidate of their own to replace you. So, whatever happens, the Wydvilles will never achieve absolute power over England. Their time has come and gone."

"And who told you that?" I hissed at him. This was getting irritating.

"Your niece, Richard, your niece, Elizabeth." Richard got up, came over to my window embrasure and looked down at me threateningly:

"Are you saying Elizabeth told you something I didn't hear? As far as I could make out, she said she had to marry Henry Tudor."

"Precisely the point, Richard. All the plotting, all the murders, all the histrionics of the Wydvilles have benefited only one person ... Henry Tudor, whom they are going to make king of England." Richard sat down next to me.

"Are you saying Henry thought all this up? I didn't think he had the brains."

"No, Richard, he benefits, without having lifted a finger. He will marry Elizabeth but she will not be queen regnant, as she should be; instead Henry will make her a brood mare and that will be the extent of her power. I'm only guessing now, but I don't think you will see a Wydville as Chancellor of England or in any other position of power. Henry knows his Wydvilles and what they are capable of." Richard lowered his head. After a while, he said in a low voice:

"The kids Edward and Richard, my brother George and perhaps even Edward himself. All for the benefit of Henry Tudor, who never lifted a finger, and gets it all." What more was there to say? But there was, of course. Richard could still marry Elisabeth with the proper dispensations and I said so: Richard frowned:

"Gaius, have you any conception of how much confusion and strife would result if I suddenly married poor little Elizabeth?"

"I find it strange she did not mention her brothers at all," I replied pensively. "She affirmed she was the Yorkist heir. How much do you think she knows?" Richard shook his head.

"I can't imagine she knows but Henry sure does. I'm sorry Elisabeth has to marry this low born cad but I can't see any way out."

"Well, Richard, they'll have to kill you first, or get rid of you somehow. Impeachment!" Richard looked at me.

"And what the hell is that? Never heard it before." Because, of course, I had never said it out loud.

"It is," I said, " the destitution of a ruler from power for any number of reasons, graft, say, or profeteering and such like."

"And you think I've done any of that? Really, Gaius." I shook my head.

"Of course I don't and neither does anyone else. But that's immaterial if they want to get rid of you. I t's happened before, you know."

He sighed and got up.

"I shouldn't think that would be much of a problem, then, and the best of British luck, is all I can say." he said. "I'm off to bed." And he went. I stayed awake for a long time weighing this and that but gave up. This affair must be the most tangled bit of English history, which would be saying a lot.

19

Bosworth Field

19.1 The Night Before

Henry was just hanging out in Paris waiting for the go-ahead from the Wydvilles. Ma Wydville asked for her daughter back from court and naturally Richard sent her off, although she protested bitterly. Me, I think Richard should have married her – just imagine how many people would have survived the Tudor's favourite pastime – execution. But there you are, Richard was adamant on the matter. Me, I think he was just sick of the whole screwup.

Naturally, the Wydville faction flocked to Henry's banner. The nobles were more circumspect and many of them were still on the wall, waiting to see how things would turn out. A blow to Richard was the death of the Duke of Norfolk, one of his staunchest allies. Anyhow, a battle there must be although Richard was about to chuck the whole thing and emigrate – somewhere, anywhere. But his allies went into a panic – what would happen to them if Richard just up and left? As the man said, 'noblesse oblige'. So a battle was announced to take place at Bosworth Field in August of 1484.

I sat at the entrance to Richard's tent as dusk fell, watching the flames from the cooking fires and the guards posted on the camp perimeter. The night was to be bright with stars but there would be no moon. Not being human, I can't say what soldiers feel before a battle but for sure they have lost their survival instinct – which, as I have said before, is fight or flight.

A cat fights if he thinks he can win. He runs away if the enemy is bigger than he is. But humans no longer have this instinct or, rather, they have given it away to those who claim to be in command. Silly buggers. I went back inside and lay down on a comfy rug. There was no one in the tent but Richard and myself. There would not be much sleep for either of us tonight but that just nuts to me – I'm a nocturnal animal. As always when he is nervous, Richard was kneading his hands together.

"Well, Gaius, so here we are," he said. What can you say? I said: "Indeed."

"Tell you the truth, Gaius, I'd just as soon lose tomorrow and leave this vale of tears behind. After all, I have done what I could to keep the peace. As I have been spectacularly unsuccessful, let someone else try."

"Richard," I said, "considering the rowdies and gangsters and buccaneers you've had to deal with, it's not surprising. The only way you could have been successful was to have beheaded the lot."

"You know I couldn't have done that, Gaius," said Richard. "No matter what. It just isn't in me. I don't love power that much I would kill to get it or keep it."

"Pal, you are one in a million."

"But I've let people down, Gaius, people who believed in me, whom I should have protected." And, as if called, two transparent white figures stood before us, shimmering slightly, both fairly small. One spoke.

"Uncle," said Edward, "you promised to look after us. Why did you let them murder us?" Richard started to cry.

"Oh, my dear nephews, I did try, I did indeed. But they were too many for me."

"Gaius," said young Richard, "can you see us?" I confess I had a lump in my throat.

"Sure I can, Richard the kid. Great times we had together." Richard the ghost sighed and I continued: "I don't think what happened to you two should happen to children. But who would have guessed the evil that is in the heart of men, even your nearest and dearest. The love of power corrupts and people loose their bearings. The thirst for power is addictive and men will go to extreme ends to achieve it and even more extreme ones to keep it." The ghost Edward sighed:

"Sometime I'm happy I was spared, uncle. Those people who murdered us, I didn't want to become like them. Good bye, Uncle. Till we meet again." And they started fading.

"Don't worry, boys," sobbed Richard, "see you tomorrow."

We were obviously going to have another visitor, for the light shimmered again; this time it was a woman and a small boy. Richard sobbed even louder:

"Anne, oh, Anne and my little Edward. Why did you leave me so soon? I needed you so much. My one regret is that I spent so little time with you. Anne, why didn't I listen to you and stay in the North? We could have been happy on our estates, what did we need power for? And what good did it do us?" Anne answered:

"It was your destiny, my dear husband. How could we have known the full evil of the world and the means people will go to get what they want? In my wildest dreams, I could not have imagined it."

"Daddy," said little Edward, "when are you joining us? Mommy says it's going to be very soon." Richard tried to dry his tears.

"Soon, Edward, it will be soon indeed, why, before you know it we will all be together again."

"See you then," and he and Anne vanished. Well, that should take care of the ghosts I thought, now for a little shut eye. But two more appeared. I looked but didn't recognize them. Richard enlightened me.

"These are Henry VI and Edward, Prince of Wales. Well, my friends, if you have come to gloat, you may well do so. Tomorrow, the House of York will be no more." Henry the Prince of Wales said in his ghostly voice:

"So, tell me, Richard of York, the reason for all those battles, for all those deaths, for years of strife between our two houses that in truth knew one single ancestor?" Richard shook his head.

"My cousins, I know not. Once, I thought it was about justice. The right of kingship. But today I see it was all greed and tyranny. Would that the crown of England could disappear forever when I do." Edward continued:

"But it will not, and our strife will be repeated down the ages until the coming of Armageddon."

"Nay," I muttered. "People will come to their senses, there will be a Civil War (Crown against Parliament) and a Glorious Revolution (Protestants against Catholics) and the English will have a constitutional monarchy, a vast improvement over the current system. But it will take centuries." Edward said:

"So there is hope." I answered:

"Of sorts." Father and son faded away.

"At least," said Richard, "I won't be here for that. A consolation." Another visitor shimmered in: Richard breathed.

"Clarence. Would that you had lived; the burden was too much for me and I failed." Clarence answered:

"Richard, you could have become like our brother Edward, a tyrant and a fool, too fond of his pleasures, a man who persecuted his own kith and kin. My brother, you were tried and were not found wanting. That evil should have prevailed is the tragedy of this land." And he disappeared. Richard lay down.

"Well, Gaius, I hope that's the lot. I'm going to try to get some sleep. If Buckingham turns up, tell him I'm not receiving." I kept vigil till dawn. But we had no other visitors.

19.2 Dawn

It was dawn and all was a-bustle in Richard's tent. Knights and servers and stable boys came and went. Richard had a goblet of watered wine but wanted no food. His entourage helped him put his armour on. When he was ready, I asked:

"Aren't you going to wear your crown?" Richard raised his eyebrows.

"What for?" He asked. "I'll only get it dirty." But he put in on top of his helm, anyway. Before leaving, he turned and said:

"Well, my friend Gaius, the cat. It's been a wild race, has it not?"

"Indeed," I answered, "not a dull moment." Richard sighed.

"I could have done without some of those moments if I'd had a choice." Outside the tent, he was greeted by Sir Robert Brakenbury. They embraced.

"You needn't stay, you know," said Richard to the old man. "Go home and enjoy your old age." Sir Robert answered:

"I am a Plantagenet man, sire. What are these Tudors and Wydvilles to me? So, I will go out with the last Plantagenet." And off they went, arm in arm. When Richard was getting ready to mount his horse, another man came up to him, bowing.

"Sire, may I wish you good luck!" Richard looked up and then his eyebrows shot up in surprise.

"Sir James Tyrell! I'm afraid you've made a mistake, sir. Tudor's lines are over there." Sir James answered:

"I was ever your man, my Lord. And I will remain so till the end." Richard gasped:

"You mean that...?" but Sir James shook his head.

"No, my Lord. I was made an offer I couldn't refuse." So they galloped off together and I'm sure I didn't know what to make of it and neither, I bet, did Richard. As he was leaving, he had turned and said to me:

"Gaius, I'm off to get impeached!"

19.3 The Battle

There's not really much to say as regards the battle. Richard had the most men but, as usual in the days before national armies, most were beholden to other liege lords. And the nobility, as we both knew, had decided that they didn't want Richard and his reformist ideas on the throne of England. A good tyrant, that they knew how to deal with, but someone who cared for the rest? Oh, puleese!

Why Richard had ever trusted Stanley goes beyond anyone's comprehension. Not only was he the henpecked husband of Margaret Beaufort but he'd changed sides so many times it seems everyone had forgotten which was the side he'd been on last. Really, when Richard did behead someone, it was usually the wrong someone. They say Richard was the last of the medieval kings. Myself, I think he belonged in the century of the Civil war and the glorious revolution, a born ally of Oliver Cromwell. Was there anything more medieval that the House of Tudor?

As the opposing forces gathered with their bows and arrows, swords and what not, I climbed a nearby hill. One thing I do not like is to get blood on my coat. I can't clean it; it's too disgusting. And if I come home covered in blood, as eggs is eggs (as Richard would sasy) that flatmate of mine would insist on a bath.

So I found a convenient tree stump to look at the procedures. No prizes to guess the outcome. Anyhow, I already knew, didn't I? It's in all the history books. So I saw as Stanley changed sides and, as Richard became isolated from his own troops, one of Stanley's horsemen struck him through the chest with a long sword – I read somewhere he was a Welshman. Never liked them. As Richard fell, I closed my eyes. No one wants to see a friend die and I'd already seen too many. And when I opened them, Richard shimmered beside me.

"Richard," I said, "you're still carrying your sword and crown. You won't need them where you are going." As answer, he threw the crown into a muddy pool. Eager legs flew towards it – Henry Tudor, of course, who else. Henry picked up the crown, held it in the air in triumph and put it on his own head. All his retainers and allies cheered. What a show-off. All this reminded me of something that would happen in the distant future and couldn't help saying out loud:

"*I found* the *crown of France in the gutter and picked it up.*"[15] What a bourgeois clown! Both of them.

"What does that have to do with anything?" asked Richard, or rather, his ghost, "France wasn't part of this, not prominently, that is."

"The phrase," I said in my best schoolmaster style, "will be spoken by a Corsican upstart about five hundred years from now when he makes himself emperor of the French. The parallels are irresisteble. But you can be satisfied with the fact that an Englishman did it first!" Richard looked thoughfull:

---

[15]   Napoleon Bonaparte, Emperor of the French

"It's all humbug, you know, all this king business and courts and jewels and bowing and scraping." I nodded:

"Ceremony, the trappings of state." I said. "Take that away and what's the difference between a king and a London apprentice? The apprentice is probably smarter and has more fun. By the way, you need to throw your sword into the lake." Answer:

"Gaius, this is hardly Excalibur." A pity. I would have loved to have given Richard a Scandinavian funeral – the boat floating out to sea, the norns with their staffs, the fire. However, when I looked up to reply, Richard was gone. I thought I could see three figures walking into the mist.

I stayed where I was for a bit, looking at the festivities below, in many ways reminiscent of football fans celebrating the aftermath of their favourite team having won a decisive game on the way to the World Cup championship. I mussed to no one in particular.

"Well, Cicero, your great strategy – Cui bono – has blown a fuse. The Wydvilles committed a horrible crime to benefit someone else – Henry VII. And where are you now, you Wydvilles? You will forever remain frozen in one moment of history but otherwise forgotten... there was a sighing in the breeze and I thought I heard the words

It was pre-ordained. How else would Elizabeth have fulfilled England's destiny?

I thought about this for a while. Elizabeth? This story was full of Elizabeths. And then it struck me. Elizabeth I. Part Plantagenet, Wydville, Tudor and Boleyn. So! The last pays for all? Ask that of those who fell under Henry VII's ax or burnt in the pyres of Henry VIII and Bloody Mary!

A terrible future for England the Tudor dynasty, to my mind too great a price paid for a future Empire, greater even than that of Rome. Would the English at the time of Richard had been willing to pay the price for a glorious future? Unhappily, the price the present pay for the future is forever unknown. But I suppose they did ask for it.

The truth about Richard III, who did all the wrong things for the right reasons, will never be fully known, courtesy of Henry VII whose talent for spin exceeded even our most up-to-date spin doctors. But then he had something I'm sure our modern practitioners of the craft would love but do not have: the executioner's axe. A siringe is hardly a worthy substitute.

19.4 Aftermath

As I sat there, a mist rose slowly and the scene below me disolved. Soon I could see nothing and hear nothing. What can a cat do? Lay down for a snooze. And as I slipped into dreamland, at the back of my mind was the idea that the greatest mystery of all, which no historian has ever addressed, is: why did the English lords accept Henry VII as their overlord, giving him the power of life and death over them and all their lieges? Henry, descended from two lines of bastadry, was a true usurper. And his line extends to this day, tainting each of those who followed with bastardry.

20

The Three Comrades

ill and I were walking along the São Francisco beach towards Charitas and our favourite watering hole.

"That was a right job you did on Richard," I said and I meant it to sting. Will glanced sideways at me.

"You got a real soft spot for that bastard," was his comment. "Can't see the charm myself." I felt myself getting hot and bothered.

"Sure, Richard may have been as bad as people were in his era, but you made him bad in other ways, none of which are true or, at least, can be proven."

"Gaius, once and for all, will you get it through your skull and into that pea brain of yours that I wrote plays, not history. History is for the birds. When the legend becomes greater than the facts, believe the legend." Well, I'd heard that somewhere before but I decided not to be sidetracked by Will's broadsides. We got to our bar and our friend, Marcia, came up with the needful. We each drank and I continued:

"But you know Richard didn't do most of the things you make him do in the play. And he wasn't a hunchback. And don't quote Thomas Moore[16] at me. Moore was a Tudor lackey." Frankly, I can't feel sorry for what happened to that one. Good riddance. "And, Will, the whole play is so over the top, so grand guinol, you know." I could see Will didn't know what grand guignol was but wasn't going to bother to ask. Before we could get into another subject, a shadow fell over our table. I looked up.

---

[16]   Lord High Chancellor under Henry VIII. He died on the scaffold.

"Hi, Richard," I cried in surprise, "glad to see you. Take a weight off." Richard took a plastic chair from a nearby table and sat down. He was just as I had seen him last although he now wore a pair of jeans, a local soccer club T-shirt and flip-flops.

"Thought I'd just pass by. Can you get me a beer, Gaius? Don't know the lingo." Will answered before I could.

"You don't need any lingo here, chum. Just wave a finger or, rather wave two as I'm ready for another, and the beer will appear." Richard waved two fingers and, before you could say *knife,* the foaming glasses where there. Will took up his and said:

"By the way, I'm William Shakespeare."

"Thought you might be," answered Richard looking at Will a bit askance. "I should really be mad at you for writing that appalling rubbish about me. Why, there are so many holes in the story ..."

"Yes, yes," I interrupted, "you could ride all the king's horses through them. But Will doesn't care, do you,Will?" Will looked gruff:

"Damn right I don't," came his answer. "It's entertainment, for God's sake, not a bloody history lesson." He took a slurp. "And, anyway, I probably made you more famous than any other king in English history." Richard sneered:

""A horse, a horse, my kingdom for a horse!' Oh, pulseese!" Will looked a mite contrite. He said lamely:

"It sounded good. I was much praised. Everyone liked it!" Richard went on, still on a roll:

"If I'd wanted a horse, I'd have kicked off one of the troopers to get it."

Well, I wasn't about to get into the merits or demerits of Will's *Richard III.* But I did have now bit to add:

"How much did they pay you, Will, for the lines:

> *'now civil wounds are stopp'd, peace lives again*
> *That she may long live here'*

After all, you were describing the bloody – taken literally – Tudors!" Willi growled:

"None of your damn business." I snickered. Everyone has their price, even Will Shakespeare. Richard and I exchanged glances and snickered. To bury the hatchet, I lifted my glass, we clinked and Richard said:

"You know, I've had lots of time to think about everything. Sir James Tyrrel was a faithful Tudor retainer for many years. But in the end, he confessed to the murders of the boys."

I asked:

"Why did he do that?" It was Will who answered:

"Took him long enough, didn't it? About 20 years or so after the fact." Richard ignored both of us:

"But the strange thing is, Tyrell never told them where the bodies where. Or, if he did, no one ever bother to dig 'em up."

"Or, perhaps," I added, "Henry didn't want to know or care."

"Nonsense, Gaius," replied Richard impatiently. "Had he had the bodies, everything would become clear as daylight, the poor boys could be buried decently and it would be all clear sailing for Monsieur Henri. Instead, for years men and boys turned up claiming to be either Edward or Richard. Must have been a real nuisance." William scratched his chin and I straightened my whiskers.

"You know," said Will, "you may have something there, Richard. Tyrell's revenge, perhaps."

"Truth to tell," I interrupted, "the whole episode is so covered in spin and lies and special interests that, at this point, it's impossible to separate fact from fiction. So let's forget it all and have another drink."

The sun was slowly disappearing behind the city of Rio, leaving the sky glowing with blue and all shades of pink and violet; the skyscrapers' lights came on like a firework display; fairy lights twinkled along the runway of the Santos Dumont airport. The sun's last rays skimmed towards us, dancing across the waters of Guanabara Bay. And we had another drink.

21

The Richard Paradox

A **paradox** is a statement that apparently contradicts itself. Here, we are looking at the paradox of a person who, by all accounts and purposes was good during one portion of his life but because utterly evil during another, in fact, changed from good to evil to a degree where we might have to say he was another person altogether. Where there two Richard III? A Duke Jekell and King Hyde? Did Richard have a split personality? Was he bipolar? And where was King Hyde during Duke Jekyll's life in the north of England?

Richard was born in 1452, the youngest son of Richard, Duke of York and Cecily Neville. He participated in the battles of Barnet and Tewkesbury when he was about 18 and had previously followed his brother king Edward into exile when fleeing the Lancastrian army. He later negotiated a truce between his brothers Edward and George, persuading George to return to the Yorkist side.

Edward IV had great faith in his brother Richard, Duke of Gloucester, who had proven his loyalty and skill as a military commander. In 1469, he was named Constable of England, Great Chamberlain and Lord High Admiral.

Richard controlled the North of England until Edward IV's death. Especially in York, he was much loved for his community services; he also raised the churches of Middleham and Barnard Castle to collegiate status. In fact, in York he is still a hero to this day.

Suddenly, as if at the wave of a wand, once Richard arrived in London and, following his brother's funeral, he turns into a ravening monster – king Hyde. He orders torture for the sake of torture, beheadings at the drop of a hat, usurps the English crown from his nephew Edward V and murders this nephew and his brother, children of about 12 1and 10 years of age, in the Tower of London. So what happened to the Duke Jekyll who had left York for London?

Most of what we know about the crimes of King Hyde comes from the time of the Tudors who had reasons enough to blacken Richard's character as much as they could, hiding behind Richard a multitude of sins of their own. As the Americans say, all evidence from time of the Tudors should be regarded as *fruit of the poisonous tree*. The Tudor allegations cannot be proven (or disproven, for that matter).

So what do we know about Richard's actual misdeeds as King Hyde:

- He did take the throne from his nephew Edward.
- He did execute diverse gentlemen from the Wydville family.
- He did order the executions of Lord Hastings and the Duke of Buckingham.

But there are other things he could have done to make his position more secure that he did not do:

- He did not declare attainder or execute Lord Stanley, a known changer of sides and an obvious threat to him as Henry Tudor's step-father.
- He did not declare attainder or harm in any way on Margaret Beaufort although she was up to her ears in Buckingham's rebellion. Instead, he passed Margaret's estates to her husband, Lord Stanley.
- He did not move against the dowager Queen Elisabeth or her daughters and he did not touch her estates.
- He did not marry his niece, Elizabeth of York.

So, on the one hand we have a prince who ruled well, was interested in the lot of the lower classes and higher learning. His interest in printing as a means of making knowledge available to all citizens is another point in his favor (this is part of his message to the

House of Commons that included other statutes directly improving the life of the communality.)

All in all, on the evidence we have, Richard would have been a vast improvement over Henry Tudor, a mean little man with his way to make. In fact, Henry VII revoked all the statutes in Richard's agenda to the House of Commons.

22

The Princes' Fate

For centuries the question has raged: what happened to Edward IV's heir, Edward V, and his brother. Were they smuggled abroad or were they indeed killed in the Tower. There is no answer so all solutions are legitimate.

Herein is given one solution. Take it or leave it. The truth will never be known.

By the way, in the 1700s two skeletons of what were definitely boys were found in a hitherto blocked off part of the Tower. DNA analysis could today establish who their were. Unfortunately, Queen Elizabeth II has not allowed the bodies to be exhumed.

Let us hope that the next English monarch will approve the exhumation and we will get partial answers to all our questions. One question, though, will remain: if these are the princes, who put them under the stairs?

Appendix I – Impeachment in England

If impeachment means the removal of a head of state for having committed high crimes and misdemeaners, there haave been quite a few cases thoughout English history. I am not asserting that any on the kings listed below have actually committed high crimes and/or misdemeanors, but that's hardly the point if you want to get rid of a king for whatever reason.

- Let us take as our first case: Edward II (1284-1337): Edward was gay and he had the misfortune, or she did, to be married to a French princess who would later be known as 'the she-wolf of France'. She and her lover impeached Edward and ruled for his son Edward III until his majority (another child king). The methodology used for Edward II's impeachment was assassination.
- Richard II (1367-1400?) – another child king who grew up to be a bad ruler and, worst, a bad general. After a disasterous campaign in Ireland he was impeached by his cousin, Henry of Bollingbroke, who took the title of Henvy IV. To ensure Richard could not cause more trouble, he too was assassinated; the exact date remains unknown.

- Richard III (1452-1485) – is there anything more to say about him? His enemies enveloped themselves in moral causes and got rid of him in battle.
- Charles I (1600-1649) – Chales claimed to rule by divine right and the English would have none of it. Parliament rose against him, captured him and condemned him. He had his head cut off.
- James II (1633-1701) – he, too, wanted to rule by divine right and to add insult to injury, became a Catholic. He was kicked out and never let back in. His two daughters took his place, the first one, MaryII, married a victorious general, William of Orange, who certainly helped things on: the English called the affair 'the glorious revolution'. James II and his heirs were allowed to gnaw on their bitterness in exile.

Well, that should really be the lot but there is another curious case that might well be seen as impeachment.

- Edward VIIII (1894-1972) – this was called an abdication but might as well have been an impeachment; Edward was condemned for consorting with an enemy agent, exiled and made miserable whenever he returned to his native land.[17]

So, there you are. As William Shakespeare would have said:
A rose by any other name would smell as sweet (or bitter?)

As you might say, the outcome is the same although nowadays they have a proper name for it – impeachment.

---

[17]   The American, Wallis Simpson

Appendix II – Richard III's Parliament

R ichard II reigned for 777 days. His Parliament sat from 23 January to 22 February 1584. The resulting legislation was the first to be published in English and the first to be printed. Statutes were divided into private and public.

Private statutes:

1st - *Titulus Regius*: Richard of Gloucester declared king and his son, Edward, heir apparent. Edward V and his brother Richard declared illegitimate due to Edward's pre-contract to Lady Eleanor Butler.

2nd to 18th: Attainders relating to Buckingham's rebellion. Men considered leader had their lands confiscated; Inheristance claims\benefits to individuals: Francis, Viscount Lovell, Sir James Tyrell. Return of lands to the house of Percy.

Public Statutes:

1st, 5th and 7th: Protection for buyers' of land – to safeguard against fraudulent practices, all transfers had to be made through appropriate courts.

3rd: Bail for suspected felons, protecting them for improsionment before trial.

4th: Minimum property qualifications for jurors, with the objective of making them less open to bribery.

6th: Reduction of the powers of the 'Piedpower courts' to their original jurisdiction (offences committed at fairs).

8th: Prevention of commercial dishonesty in the cloth trade.

9th: Regulated import and export of goods and exempting the pirnting and selling of books

10th: Prohibited importation of silk lace, scissor, bells, nails, etc.

11th: Italian merchants to import ten good bow staves with every butt of malmsey.

12th: Prohibited importantion of ready made good.

13th: Wine and oil sold only after being measured with the prices controlled.

14th: Dismes: the 10th of all spiritual livings given to the king, charging clerics to do the collection.

15th: Resumption of all grants and estates to Elizabeth Grey, based upon the *Titulus Regius*.

Appendix III - Titulus Regius[xi]

To the High and Mighty Prince,
Richard, Duc of Gloucester

"Please it youre Noble Grace to understande the consideracon, election, and petition of us the lords spiritual and temporal and commons of this reame of England, and thereunto agreably to geve your assent, to the common and public wele of this lande, to the comforts and gladnesse of all the people of the same.

"First, we considre how that heretofore in tyme passed this lande many years stode in great prosperite, honoure, and tranquillite, which was caused, foresomuch as the kings then reignyng used and followed the advice and counsaill of certaine lords speulx and temporelx, and othre personnes of approved sadnesse, prudence, policie, and experience, dreading God, and havyng tendre zele and affection to indifferent ministration of justice, and to the comon and politique wele of the land; then our Lord God was dred, luffed (loved), and honoured; then within the land was peace and tranquillite, and among neghbors concorde and charite; then the malice of outward enemyes was mightily repressed and resisted, and the land honourably defended with many grete and glorious victories; then the entrecourse of merchandizes was largely used and exercised; by ehich things above remembered, the land was greatly enriched soo that as wele the merchants and artificers as other poor people, laboryng for their lyvyng in diverse occupations, had competent gayne to the sustentation of thaym and their households, livyng without miserable and intolerable povertie. But afterward, when that such as had the rule and governaunce of this land, deliting in adulation and flattery and lede by sensuality and concupiscence, followed the counsaill of persons insolent, vicious, and of inordinate avarice, despising the counsaill of good, vertuous, and prudent personnes such as above be remembred, the prosperite of this land dailie decreased soo that felicite was turned into miserie, and prosperite into adversite, and the ordre of polecye, and of the law of God and man, confounded; whereby it is likely this reame to falle into extreme miserie and desolation, - which God defende, - without due provision of convenable remedie bee had in this behalfe in all godly hast.

"Over this, amonges other thinges, more specifially we consider howe that the tyme of the raigne of King Edward IV, late decessed, after the ungracious pretensed marriage, as all England hath cause to say, made betwitx the said King edward IV and Elizabeth, sometyme wife to Sir John Grey, Knight, late nameing herself and many years heretofore Queene of England, the ordre of all politeque rule was perverted, the laws of God and of Gode's church, and also the lawes of nature, and of England, and also the laudable customes and liberties of the same, wherein every Englishman is inheritor, broken, subverted, and contempned, against all reason and justice, so that this land was ruled by self-will and pleasure, feare and drede, all manner of equite and lawes layd apart and despised, whereof ensued many inconvenients and mischiefs, as murdres, estortions, and oppressions, namely of pooe and impotent people, so that no man was sure of his lif, land, ne lyuvelode, ne of his wif, doughter, no servannt, every good maiden and woman standing in drede to be ravished and defouled. And besides this, what discords, inward battailes, effusion of Christian men's blode, and namely, by the destruction of the noble blode of this lond, was had and comitted within the same, it is evident and notarie through all this reaume unto the grete sorrowe and heavynesse of all true Englishmen. And here also we considre howe the said pretensed marriage, betwitx the above named King Edward the Elizabeth Grey, was made of grete presumption, without the knowyng or assent of the lords of this londe, and alsoe by sorcerie and wiche-crafte, committed by the said Elizabeth and her moder, Jacquett Duchess of Bedford, as the common opinion of the peole and the publique voice, and fame is through all this land; and hereafter, if and as the case shall require, shall bee proved sufficiently intyme and place convenient. And here also we considre how that the said pretenced marriage was made privately and secretly, with edition of banns, in a private chamber, a profane place, and not openly in the face of the church, aftre the laws of Godd's churche, but contrarie thereunto, and the laudable custome of the Churche of England. And how also, that at the tyme of the contract of the same pretensed marriage, and bifore and longe tyme after, the saide King Edw was and stood marryed and troth plyght to oone Dame Elianor Butteler, doughter of the old Earl of Shrewsbury, with whom the said King Edward had made a precontracte of matronie, long tyme bifore he made the said pretensed mariage with the said Elizabeth Grey in manner and fourme aforesaid. Which premises being true, as in veray trouth they been true, it appeareth and followeth evidently, that the said King Edward duryng his lyfe and the said Elizabeth lived together sinfully and dampnably in adultery, against the lawe of God and his church; and therefore noe marvaile that the souverain lord and head of this londe, being of such ungodly disposicion, and provokyng the ire and indignation of oure Lorde God, such haynous mischiefs and inconvenients as is above remember, were used and committed in the reame amongst the subjects. Also it appeareth evidently and followeth that all th'issue and children of the said king been bastards, and unable to inherite or to clayme anything by inheritance, by the lawe and custome of England.

"Moreover we consider howe that afterward, by the thre estates of this reame assembled in a parliament holden at Westminster the 17th. yere of the regne of the said King Edward theiiijth, he than being in possession of the coroune and roiall estate, by an acte made in the same parliament, George Duc of Clarence, brother to the said King Edward now decessed, was convicted and attainted of high treason; as in the same acte is conteigned more at large. Because and by treason whereof all the issue of the said George was and is disables and barred of all right and clayme that in any wise they might have or challenge by inheritance to the crowne and roiall dignitie of this reame, by the auncien lawe and custome of this same reame.

"Over this we consider howe that ye be the undoubted sonne and heire Richard late Duke of Yorke verray enheritour to the said crowne and dignitie roiall and as in right Kyng of Englond by way to enheritaunce and that at this time the premisses duelly considered there is noon other peron lyving but ye only, that by right may clayme the said coroune and dignitie roiall, by way of enhertiaunce, and how that ye be born within this lande, by reason whereof, as we deme in our myndes, ye be more naturally enclyned to the prosperitie and comen weal of the same: and all the three estates of the land have, and may have more certain knowledge of your birth and filiation above said. Wee considre also, the greate wytte, prudence, justice, princely courage, and the memorable and laudable acts in diverse battalls which we by experience know ye heretofore have done for the salvacion and defence of this same reame, and also the great noblesse and excellence of your byrth and blode as of hym that is descended of the thre most royal houses in Christendom, that is to say, England, Fraunce, and Hispaine.

"Wherefore these premisses by us diligently considered, we desyring affectuously the peas, tranquilitie and wele publique of this lande, and the reduction of the same to the auncien honourable estate, and prosperite, and havyng in your greate prudence, justice, princely courage and excellent virtue, singular confidence, have chosen in all that is in us is and by this our wrytyng choise you, high and myghty Prynce into our Kyng and souveraine lord &c., to whom we know for certayn it appertaneth of enheritaunce so to be choosen. And hereupon we humbly desire, pray, and require your said noble grace, that accordinge to this election of us the three estates of this lande, as by your true enheritaunce ye will accept and take upon you the said crowne and royall dignitie with all things thereunto annexed and apperteyning as to you of right belongyng as well by enheritaunce as by lawful election, and in case ye do so we promitte to serve and to assist your highnesse, as true and faithfull subjietz and liegemen and to lyve and dye with you in this matter and every other just quarrel. For certainly we bee determined rather to adventure and comitte us to the perill of our lyfs and jopardye of death, than to lyve in such thraldome and bondage as we have lyved long tyme heretofore, oppressed and injured by new extorcos and imposicons, agenst the lawes of God and man, and the liberte, old polce and lawes of this reame wherein every Englishman is inherited. Our Lorde God Kyng of all Kynges by whose infynyte goodnesse and eternall providence all thyngs have been pryncypally gouverned in this worlde lighten your soule, and graunt you grace to do, as well in this matter as in all other, all that may be accordyng to his will and pleasure, and to the comen and publique wele of this land, so that after great cloudes, troubles, stormes, and tempests, the son of justice and of grace may shyne uppon us, to the comforte and gladnesse of all true Englishmen.

"Albeit that the right, title, and estate, whiche our souverain lorde the Kynge Richard III hath to and in the crown and roiall dignite of this reame of England, with all things thereunto annexed and appertynyng, have been juste and lawefull, as grounded upon the lawes of God and of nature and also upon the auncien lawes and laudable customes of this said reame, and so taken and reputeed by all such personnes as ben lerned in the above-saide laws and custumes. Yet, neverthelesse, forasmoche as it is considred that the most parte of the people of this lande is not suffisiantly lerned in the abovesaid lawes and customes whereby the trueth and right in this behalf of liklyhode may be hyd, and not clerely knowen to all the people and thereupon put in doubt and question: And over this howe that the courte of Parliament is of suche autorite, and the people of this lande of suche nature and disposicion, as experience teacheth that maifestation and declaration of any trueth or right made by the thre estats of this reame assembled in parliament, and by auctorite of the same maketh before all other thyng, moost faith and certaintie; and quietyng men's myndes, remoweth the occasion of all doubts and seditious language:

"Therefore at the request, and by the assent of the three estates of this reame, that is to say, the lords spuelx and temporalx and comens of this lande, assembled in this present parliament by auctorite of the same, bee it pronounced, decreed and declared, that our said souveraign lorde the kinge was and is veray and undoubted kyng of this reame of Englond; with all thyngs thereunto within this same reame, and without it annexed unite and apperteynyng, as well by right of consanguinite and enheritance as by lawful election, consecration and coronacion. And over this, that at the request, and by the assent and autorite abovesaide bee it ordeigned, enacted and established that the said crowne and roiall dignite of this reame, and the inheritaunce of the same, and other thyngs thereunto within the same reame or without it annexed, unite, and now apperteigning, rest and abyde in the person of our said souveraign lord the kyng during his lyfe, and after his decesse in his heires of his body begotten. And in especiall, at the request and by the assent and auctorite abovesaid, bee it ordeigned, enacted, established, pronounced, decreed and declared that the high and excellent Prince Edward, sone of our said souveraign lorde the Kyng, be heire apparent of our said souveraign lorde the kyng, to succeed hym in the abovesaid crown and roiall dignite, with all thyngs as is aforesaid thereunto unite annexed and apperteignyng, to have them after the decease of our saide souveraign lorde the kyng to hym and to his heires of his body lawfully begotten."

Endnotes

ⁱ Henry Tudor, Lancastrian pretender to the English throne

ⁱⁱ A red horse went out; and to him who sat on it, it was granted to take peace from the earth, and that men would slay one another; and a great sword was given to him. (New Testament: The Four horses of the Apocalypse).

ⁱⁱⁱ Henry Strafford, 2nd Duke of Buckingham. His family had been on the side of Lancaster; when Henry became Duke, at the age of 6, Edward IV took charge of him; he was married to a sister of Elisabeth Wydville at the age of 12.

^{iv} Sir Thomas Stanley, first married to Eleanor Neville, sister of Warwick, the king maker (father to Anne, Richard's wife), then to Margaret Beaufort, mother of the Lancastrian pretender, Henry Tudor. Stanley therefore had a foot in both camps.

^v Margaret Beaufort, Countess of Richmond, a descendent of John of Gaunt on the distaff side; John of Gaunt was father of Henry IV, grandfather of Henry V and great-grandfather of Henry VI.

^{vi} American Constitution, 5th Amendment - Sets out rules for indictment by grand jury and eminent domain, protects the right to due process, and prohibits self-incrimination and double jeopardy

^{vii} William, Lord Hastings, loyal to the Yorkist cause. He had a seat on Edward IV's council, and was the King's Chamberlain and had a baronage. He was named governor of Calais, a post coveted by Lord Rivers, the Queen's brother. This, and his habit of aiding and abetting Edward IV in his womanizing, earned him a stay in the Tower of London.

^{viii} Edward IV first became king in 1461. However, a Lancastrian army invaded England in September 1470 and Edward fled to the Netherlands. Edward's later reign, from 1471 to 1483 was a period of relative peace and security.

^{ix} François Marie August, Voltaire (1694-1778). Candide.

^x Edward would be executed by Henry Tudor (1499) as demanded by the Spanish sovereigns so Henry's son, Arthur, could marry a princess of Spain; Margaret was executed as an old lady (1541) by Henry VIII for reasons unknown.

^{xi} I have included the Titulus Regulus as it was written at the time (in the 15th century)